Rebellious

Portrait of a Woman
Book 3

Kari Lee Harmon

PUBLISHER'S NOTE: This is a work of fiction. Names, characters, places, and incidents either are the product of the author's imagination or are used fictitiously. Any resemblance to actual persons, living or dead, business establishments, events, or locales is entirely coincidental.

Cover art by Dar Albert at Wicked Smart Designs

Published by Oliver-Heber Books

0 9 8 7 6 5 4 3 2 1

This book is dedicated to all the women who have been misunderstood in one way or another. Know that you are seen and heard. There is a place for us all in this big, ole world 😉 This one is for you, ladies!

Chapter One

re·bel·lious

ADJECTIVE

Resisting treatment or management

"Hey, Peter, what made you change your mind?" I smiled wide.

Opening the door, I resisted the urge to yank him inside. This was the first date I'd had in far too long. I'd lit some incense candles in my apartment above my New Age shop, *Peace, Love, and Harmony*, wanting to set the mood.

I couldn't afford for anything to go wrong this time.

Peter Sherman pushed his glasses further up his nose, looking around warily as he stepped inside my apartment and wiped the snow off his boots but didn't take them off. He left his coat on as well and smoothed his combover haircut the blustery wind had messed.

He cleared his throat before answering my question. "My mother."

"Great!" I said a little too enthusiastically to cover my inward groan.

Our mothers both belonged to the Bedazzled Boomers group and had been trying to fix us up for months. Peter had been on board at first, until the rumors started. I hadn't been on board until recently after all the men in town started avoiding me as if I had a venereal disease. Peter wasn't exactly my type, but what could I say...I was lonely.

Which made me desperate.

It was early January. Where was my fresh start? I had turned forty right after the new year, and for some reason, this birthday was hitting me hard. Two of my best friends, Zoe and Tiffany, had already turned forty. The last member of our four musketeers, Morticia, who ran her father's funeral home, wouldn't turn forty until the summer. She still had time for good luck to strike her like it had the others.

Great things had come their way.

Zoe's wedding was in just over one month, on Valentine's Day, to our very own Dr. Chaz Anderson. The four of us had grown up together in high school and met on the cheer squad. Chaz, aka Chucky the Dorkmeister, was four years younger than us and the waterboy for the football team.

He'd had the biggest crush on Zoe back then, but they hadn't gotten together until two years after Zoe's husband of twenty years and father to their four children left to go backpacking across the U.S. to find himself. Since then, she'd taken her catering business to the next level as a full-service party planner and taken another chance on love with Chaz.

Then Tiffany, who taught sensual massage for a living, had her wealthy Grammy die, leaving her everything, causing her ex-husband, estranged parents, and twin sister to come out of the woodwork. She spiraled into a mid-life crisis and slept with our local Irish pub owner, Matthew McGinnis, resulting in adorable twins born on New Year's Day. They were now happier than ever and engaged to be married next summer.

I, on the other hand, was apparently cursed.

"Ms. Jones, what are you doing?"

I blinked, startled from my daydream. "Oh, dude. My bad." I released the trigger to extinguish the flame from my utility lighter with the extended nozzle. Grabbing the fire-resistant cloth that I kept nearby, I threw it over the table-cloth I'd just set on fire.

"My God..." was all he said.

"PeeWee...I mean, Peter, why so formal? Ms. Jones is my mother. Call me Harmony, or just Harm." I headed to the kitchen as if starting fires was a normal occurrence for me and popped open two beers, then turned back to find him scanning my apartment with bugged-out eyes.

I took a big swig, handing him the other bottle.

He ignored my hand, taking a wary step back.

Here we go. I tried not to roll my eyes.

He gaped at the scene before him. "W-What is all this?"

I'd dedicated a rich, wooden stand to use as an altar to place my tools, symbols, and other items that helped me focus my energy and intention for the rituals I performed. I'd performed tonight's ritual for love just before Peter got here. I wasn't an expert in anything, but I enjoyed exploring different processes.

I used red and pink candles to represent the energy of attraction and affection. Crystals like rose quartz, garnet, and rhodonite enhanced love, romance, and emotional healing. I scattered herbs and flowers like rose petals, lavender, jasmine, and other herbs associated with love and desire about. I had even placed symbols and figurines associated with love like Venus, Aphrodite, and hearts to invoke their energy. I figured we needed all the help we could get.

Personal items like a piece of my jewelry and a photograph of Peter helped me connect our energies, and I'd added a note with written intentions for my desired outcome for our date. And finally, I'd burned incense like rose, sandalwood, and patchouli to create a calming atmosphere and to draw in our love energies. I really didn't see what the big deal was.

"Funny you should ask..." I bit my lip as I sashayed toward him, trying to salvage the evening.

He hopped a good foot back.

"Don't be afraid, babe. This is just a simple little altar. It's all good, I promise."

"It's all crazy, is what it is." The judgmental, horrified look on his face was one I had seen far too often lately.

"Peter, it's harmless. Just something to set the mood. I'm—"

"I know what you are. The rumors are true. You're a witch. You're trying to cast a spell on me."

"I don't proclaim to be a witch, although I am fascinated by modern witchery. You don't have to worry. I don't go around casting spells on people. I simply dabble in the practice a little bit for my own benefit by combining different traditions, using elements of folk magic, herbalism, astrology, and other esoteric practices. I use my magical practices for good, not evil, like influencing an event, bringing good fortune, protection, love, and healing in my own life, but I can see setting a little ambiance was a mistake. Let's start over. Let me hang your coat for you." I reached out and touched his arm. That was all.

One. Light. Touch.

He let out a high-pitched scream, jerking his violated limb from the garment as he tore out of my apartment and flew down my stairs. His coat snagged on a hook and ripped, hanging half off his gangly body.

He shrieked, "I've been attacked! Call Officer Pickles, stat!"

"Peter, wait!" I quickly followed to no avail.

Coming to a stop on the sidewalk, I wrapped my arms over my Princess Leia Star Wars t-shirt, shivering in the frigid winter night air. I'd even parted my short hair down the middle, swirling both sides with gel into circles—my version of the Leia buns—instead of my usual spikes in hopes that PeeWee Sherman would be my Han Solo.

I sighed. Looked like all I got was solo—minus Han—with another night spent alone.

"Was that...?" One of my middle brothers, Harry, walked out of my shop down below and locked the door.

He'd agreed to cover for me so I could entertain. With a family our size, it's what we did whenever any of us needed a favor. He had darker red hair than my auburn, but all eight of us had the same pale green cat eyes. I was the only girl and the youngest.

Yay me.

Yet another reason why men steered clear of me. I grimaced. "You guessed it. That was my date."

He looked at me and arched one brow high. "Peter Sherman? He's a nice enough guy, but he doesn't seem like your usual type."

"Desperate times." I shook my head. "Don't ask."

He gave me the once over. "Interesting outfit."

"A little role playing that didn't work out."

"It seems so." He grunted. "What was with the screaming and his ripped clothes hanging off him?"

"He freaked out over my altar and screamed when I offered to take his coat. It snagged on a hook on his way out. It was literally nothing."

"That didn't look like *nothing* to me." He shook his head. "Appearances are everything, Harm, and this isn't the first time that something like this has happened. People are going to believe the rumors that you're a sex-addicted witch casting spells to bend men to your will are true if you're not careful. This needs to stop."

"I agree, this does need to stop. I'm not going to rest until I figure out who is spreading these rumors. It's not fair. I'm not doing anything wrong. I'm not even asking for marriage or children. I just want a companion. Why is that so wrong?"

"It's not wrong, Harm." He slid his huge hands into his pockets, standing larger than life above me. "We all just think you're going about it the wrong way."

"*We?*" It made me feel horrible that even my own family didn't believe me. "Let me guess, Mom put a bug in your ear to talk to me."

"She didn't have to. I volunteered." He studied me with a deep crease between his eyes. "I'm worried about you. We all are."

"Well don't be. I'll just get a cat...or four. I'm done trying. The Love Boat has sailed off into the sunset, and I'm not on it. My venture into romance is officially over."

My brother eyed me shrewdly as if he could predict the future, and I got chills when he said, "I've learned to trust the niggling feeling in my gut, and it tells me your troubles have only just begun."

"THIS CAN'T BE HAPPENING. I'm innocent, Zander." I raised my chin defiantly as I sat in a courtroom before the honorable Zander Jackson.

Damn Harry's gut.

There'd been a cancelation in the court system, so Zander had squeezed my case in a couple days later. Half the town had shown up to watch my fall from grace, with Heather Hunnicut sitting front and center, loving every minute of this. The five-foot, platinum-blonde Barbie doll has had a crush on Peter since the fifth grade. She was way out of his league if you asked me, yet he'd never asked her out.

I think she scared the wee out of him.

"I'll be the judge of your innocence, Ms. Jones." Zander narrowed his dark gaze at me. "And it's Judge Jackson to you."

I went to high school with Zander. Had even gone on a date with him back in the day. It hadn't ended well, which didn't help my case now. I still couldn't believe PeeWee Sherman had pressed charges against me. The men in town had convinced him the *man attacks* had to stop, so he needed to press charges for sexual harassment.

It was so unfair.

If I had wanted to attack him, he would know it. I'd barely touched him. He'd ripped his jacket all on his own in his Gumby scramble to get away from me. And now I found myself in a fine Howdy Doody mess.

"You're not innocent." Peter surged to his feet, back rigid and hands fisted. "You're a crazy witch!" He thrust a long, bony finger at me.

Zander pounded his gavel on the podium. "Sit down, Mr. Sherman. I will have order in my courtroom."

Peter sat reluctantly, with a pout on his gaunt face. "She has a whole shrine, I tell you. She put a spell on me. See?" He pointed to a pimple on his chin. "I haven't had pimples since puberty."

"With the way you're acting, I'd say you're still a child, PeeWee." I shook my head, disgusted with myself for ever giving him a chance. Had I really grown that desperate? Why wouldn't anyone give *me* a chance? Was I really that awful to spend an evening with? It was giving me a complex.

"Is this true?" Zander raised a brow at me.

I shrugged. "I mean, if the pimple fits..."

He leveled an unamused gaze at me and repeated more firmly, "Do you have a shrine, Ms. Jones?"

I sighed, so over the reactions my hobbies instilled. What was the big deal regarding my beliefs? I came across all sorts of interesting things in my line of work that intrigued me to explore more. Since when was that a bad thing?

"I own a New Age shop. I have all sorts of things in my store. You know that, *Judge Jackson.*"

He paused a beat and just stared at me with a sleek, black raised brow. "I'm not talking about your shop. I'm talking about your apartment. Answer the question. Are you a witch, and did you cast a spell on Mr. Sherman?"

The courtroom turned deathly quiet.

"Peter has a pimple because he stressed himself out, *not* because of anything I did. I'm not a witch. I have hobbies. I dabble in lots of things for myself," I clarified and looked at Peter as if I were talking to a child. "I seek knowledge of all sorts of things for myself. That's harmless and not a crime."

"Why did you have the shrine set up?" Zander spoke again, drawing my gaze back to his suspicious one.

For the love of goddesses everywhere.

I could feel my face flush with heat and threw up my hands in defeat. "Look, it's no secret I've been having trouble in the romance department. I was desperate enough to accept a date my mother set up." I gave my mother, Wanda Jones, a pointed look, making it clear that she was in part at fault as well, then I looked back at Zander. "No offense to PeeWee, but we're not exactly the best match."

Peter let out a harsh laugh and smoothed his combover, muttering, "Ya think?" He glared at me. "For the last time, the name is Peter."

"I'm not looking for forever," I went on, ignoring his comment. "I was just looking for a good time." I lifted one shoulder. "I was only trying to set the mood for a successful evening to help enhance our passion. Though I now see that even a dozen oysters and an entire bottle of Viagra couldn't have helped our situation." I raised my hands, palms up. "That was all there was to it."

"Apparently, that was enough." Judge Jackson frowned. "Mr. Sherman isn't the first man to complain about your rather unusual tactics to secure *companionship.* It should come as no surprise to you that the men banded together to do something about it."

"Yes, I'm a little much for some people, but different doesn't have to be bad." Who was I kidding? We were talking about a small, traditional, old-fashioned town like Mayflower, Massachusetts. "Look, I can honestly say I've never harassed or attacked anyone. I can't help it I'm misunderstood."

"Majority rules, Ms. Jones." Zander stared me down with his serious judge expression. "Get help or go to jail."

"Lock her up." Peter's voice cracked as he pushed his glasses up his nose. "She's dangerous. All the men say so."

"You're not exactly innocent, Peter." Beverly Sherman sat up straighter in her bedazzled jean jacket and stared disapprovingly at her son. "You didn't even give the poor girl a chance. You could have said no to a date with her if you didn't want to go that badly."

I liked the woman.

"Exactly. I don't know what you're so afraid of, Peter. I don't bite...unless you ask me to." I smirked, sick of the male species in general. "All you had to do was say no, *babe*. It's really not that difficult." I leaned back in my chair and crossed my arms, my smirk gone as I stared him down with all the frustration I felt.

It was *his* fault we were in this situation right now.

"And all *you* had to do was act like a lady." My mother sat next to Beverly, wearing a matching bedazzled jacket, and leveled a hard, disappointed look at me. No matter how old I became, that look had always made me second guess myself.

Okay, so maybe it was my fault a little, I admitted to myself, but still...

"I'm not a lady, Mother, and frankly, I'm tired of you trying to make me into one." I was a tomboy, and always had been. What did she expect from me with seven older brothers? I hadn't been *girly* a day in my life, but I liked who I was. I just wanted to find a man who liked who I was as well.

"You're right. You're not a lady. You're a wild child, and therein lies the problem. *This* is why you're in trouble. You need help taming your impulses." My mother tsked after speaking loud enough for the entire court room to hear. "Your father and brothers and I are worried about you."

Beverly squeezed her hand in support.

My father frowned from the row behind them by my brothers.

I slid down in my seat.

"For the last time, I am not a sex addict." I ground my teeth. They had no idea what it was like to be me, especially over the past year.

"Your actions say otherwise, Ms. Jones." A twinkle entered Zander's eyes, and I would swear he was enjoying this immensely. Payback for me dumping him because he was a terrible lover.

I smothered a groan of resignation, ready to call it a day and take my punishment. "What exactly do you have in mind, *Judge Jackson?*"

"Attend SAA." His lips tipped up a smidgen.

My brow puckered. "SAA?"

"The Sex Addicts Anonymous program."

I gaped.

PeeWee smirked.

The mothers gasped.

Zander continued. "You follow the 12-step approach to help you achieve and maintain sexual sobriety and recovery. In SAA, the steps involve admitting powerlessness over your addiction, seeking help from a higher power, making amends, and helping others with the same addiction. You will attend regular meetings and be assigned a sponsor until the head therapist determines you have successfully completed the program. If you're committed and put forth the effort, you can make it through the program in a matter of months, but maintaining recovery is a lifelong process."

"I'll pass, thank you very much," I grumbled.

"Have it your way. Jail it is." The judge raised his gavel, looking overly pleased with himself.

"Wait!" My mother surged to her feet in a flurry of dazzling sparkles, reflecting the light in the courtroom as her hands moved in time with her mouth. "Please let us have a five-minute recess so we can talk to our daughter."

"My decision is—"

"Zander Jackson don't make me call your mother. I know things she doesn't...remember?" My mother gave him a look I knew all too well.

Wanda Jones was a force to be reckoned with when she wanted to be and definitely where I got my toughness from. My father, Arnold, was a lumberjack like Paul Bunyan, but the biggest softie in the county. The boys were all as big as him and we all had his red hair, but our cunningness and cat eyes were all from our mother.

Zander's gavel hovered above his podium. "Very well. Five minutes, and not one second more." He slammed his gavel down and left the courtroom, his milk chocolate cheeks not completely masking the deep red flush that had risen from his neck.

My mother, father, and seven brothers circled me to block out prying ears, all talking at once...

"What were you thinking?"

"You'll never survive jail."

"Why do you have to be different?"

"Quit embarrassing yourself."

"Our name will be scandalized."

"Your business will be ruined."

"How hard can it be?"

"Take one for the team."

"We only want what's best for you."

"Enough!" I swiped my hand through the air. "I get it, okay? God forbid, I'm the disappointment of the family for being horny."

My mother gasped.

My father cleared his throat.

My brothers stifled their laughter.

"You're not a disappointment, honey." My father patted my hand.

"But you obviously have a problem." My mother pursed her lips.

"I'm not a sex addict, Mother." I swallowed the lump in my throat, hating to show vulnerability of any kind. "I'm lonely."

My mother's face softened, and she started to say something, but Judge Jackson came out of his chambers and called the room to order. My parents and brothers returned to their seats, and everyone else sat down.

Judge Jackson looked at me. "Well, Ms. Jones, what's your sentence to be?"

"Guess I'm putting on my dancing shoes and getting to stepping. How hard can it be, right?"

"That remains to be seen." Zander's eyes narrowed suspiciously. "There's a meeting in two days, and I have the perfect sponsor in mind."

Chapter Two

Who knew Mayflower, Massachusetts, had an SAA group meeting place on the outskirts of town? It was actually located on the four corners between Mayflower and three of our neighboring towns, serving four different communities. I was never out this way, so I had no idea it even existed. Apparently, it served the AA members and several narcotic anonymous groups as well.

The go-to place for addicts in general.

I felt so out of place because I wasn't the textbook definition of an addict. I inhaled a deep breath. I would breeze through this program and graduate early to prove to everyone how wrong they were about me. Walking inside the building, I was surprised to see only five other people besides me in the meeting room with the therapist.

My face flushed as all eyes settled on me. I was the last one to arrive, and I didn't recognize anyone. I slid into my seat and looked around the room. There were three men and two women, plus me. I didn't think an SAA group would be coed on account of the nature of our addiction.

"My name is Dr. Hastings, but you can call me Shirley. I know what you're all thinking," said an older woman with pure white, short hair that was slicked back behind her ears and faded blue eyes. "Our towns are small. We don't have nearly the number of addicts as some of the other groups, so ours is coed out of necessity. But have no fear, I've assigned you each a wonderful sponsor to help you through your journey."

"We're all adults here." I rolled my eyes and stifled a snort. "I'm sure we can control ourselves." I mean, I might be horny, but that didn't mean I would jump any able body that moved.

The two women and three men all gaped at me.

"Um, hello, we're addicted to sex, remember?" One woman who was maybe twenty with a high bottle-blonde ponytail and amber eyes looked at me warily as if I were a bomb about to explode.

"How could I forget?" I sighed, resisting the urge to say, *boom*. Obviously, I was wrong. Maybe some people actually couldn't control themselves.

"Well, I *can't* forget or get back on the cheer squad until I get clean." She crossed her arms over her thick turtleneck sweater and pouted.

Good grief, Charlie Brown, I'm too old for this.

"My bad." I pretended to zip my lips and throw away the key. I just wanted to move on with my life and get this *journey* over with.

"Since you touched on why you're here, why don't we start with you." Dr. Hastings—er, Shirley—smiled.

"Hi. My name is Misty Davenport, and I am a sex addict."

"Hi, Misty," the group said as a whole except for me.

I jerked and gave her a little wave. This was just like AA in the movies. I hadn't realized we were all expected to contribute.

"I knew I had a problem when I slept with the entire football team on campus, with most of them being the boyfriends of the girls on the squad," she went on. "Not one of my finer moments, but I couldn't help myself. If you ask me, my squad members have bigger problems than me if their boyfriends are willing to cheat so easily."

"This isn't about casting blame on others, Misty." Shirley studied her and then looked at us all. "Step one is about admitting you are powerless over your addictive sexual behavior and that your lives have become unmanageable."

"You're right. I'm the one who has a problem." Misty folded her hands in her lap and looked down at the floor.

"Thank you for sharing, Misty. It takes courage to actually admit you have a problem." Shirley looked at the man beside her, who had to be seventy. "Bernard, I see you're back with us. I'm holding out hope that the third time will be the charm for you, my friend."

"Thank you, Shirley." The man had a thick head of silver hair and gray eyes. "My name is Bernard Featherwood, but you can call me Bernie."

"Hi, Bernie," everyone said, including me this time.

"I used to be a criminal defense lawyer, but I'm retired now. I've always been a sex addict, but I was single, and it never interfered with my work, so I figured what was the harm. Now that I'm retired, it has become a problem in my retirement community. You see, I've met someone. A special lady I want to commit to, but she won't say yes if I cheat. This is my third time here, and I'm hoping it's my last."

"Thank you for sharing, Bernie." Shirley nodded. "I have faith in you." She looked at the elderly woman beside Misty. "Would you care to introduce yourself next?"

"Hi. My name is Mae Chen, and I am a sex addict."

"Hi, Mae." We all knew the drill now.

The petite woman with black and gray hair in a low bun slid a pair of small round spectacles attached to a chain up onto her nose, looking like anything other than a sex addict. "I am a librarian and realized I was a sex addict by the books I was drawn to. It almost ruined my marriage because nothing is ever satisfying enough for me. My poor husband is exhausted. I'm here to get help and hopefully save my marriage before it's too late."

"We wish you the best of luck, Mae." Shirley looked at a young man in his thirties. "You're up next, sir."

"Hi there." He cleared his throat and undid the top button of his shirt. "My name is Lorenzo Gonzalez, and I am a sex addict."

"Hi, Lorenzo." We sounded like robots.

"My uncle works at the museum. He got me a job as

the night watchman. I knew I had a problem when I couldn't stop watching porn. No one was around, and I used my own device, so I didn't think it was a big deal. My uncle thought otherwise. He said get help or get out. So, that's why I'm here."

"Helping is what I'm here for." Shirley smiled and looked at the last man.

He was bald and jacked and clearly frustrated. "Hi. My name is Duke Romano, and apparently, I am a sex addict."

"Hi, Duke." Now we sounded like zombies.

"So, Romano's Bakery has been in my family for generations. My mama retired, and now I run the store. Capiche? I don't know why she got so mad when I offered coffee, tea, or me." He shrugged his massive shoulders. "Look at me. What's so wrong with me being the sweet treat? I knew I might have a problem when she told me what was wrong in five different languages. So, I'm here to get help or she said she'd give my store to my cousin Vinny." He shook his shiny head. "I said over my dead body. Capiche?"

"I think we all understand, Duke, and that's what we're here for. To help you with your problem, so you can hang onto your store." Shirley looked at me. "I guess that brings us to you, young lady."

Great. The moment I had been dreading.

I pasted on a smile and went for honesty. "Hi. My name is Harmony Jones, and I am *not* a sex addict."

"Hi, Harmony." The room chorused with far less

enthusiasm, giving me looks of pity over my perceived denial.

"What can I say? I struggle in the romance department like a lot of people. Men just don't get me. At least, the men in my town don't. When I try to show them who I am, they think I'm attacking them. I'm not. I really don't have a problem. It was either this program or jail. Honestly, I chose jail, but my family staged an intervention, basically forcing me to come here. So, that's my story."

"Well, let's hope you're not sticking to it," Shirley said. "Because you'll never get through the program if you aren't willing to try. Maybe your sponsor can help. Speaking of sponsors..." Shirley pressed a buzzer and in walked five people.

As they stood behind their chosen addict, it became apparent to me that each person had been assigned the least triggering sponsor for them. The pairings didn't act like they were attracted to each other at all. Then again, maybe that was the point. All eyes turned to me, and I shifted uncomfortably in my chair.

"Where's my sponsor?" I asked Shirley.

"Judge Jackson put in a special request that we use an old college acquaintance of his." She checked her watch and frowned.

Several moments passed, and then we heard a sound outside the door and suddenly the last sponsor walked into the room and locked eyes with me. I sucked in a sharp breath, and my heart fluttered. *Well, hell.* I suddenly realized I was dead wrong...

Looked like I had a problem after all.

"Zander Jackson doesn't know who he's messing with." I popped the top to a beer and took a big swig before I pulled the pizza and chicken wings out of the oven and carried them to the table. It had only been one week since my *date* with Peter and so much had gone wrong.

So much for my good luck!

"Why is that, doll?" Tiffany Eisenhauer took a sip of her martini, flipping her long golden-blonde waves over her shoulder as she studied me with periwinkle blue eyes. Her fiancé, Matt, was watching the twins so she could come to my apartment for our weekly girls' night.

Now, *there* was a man.

Speaking of men...

"Thick, long, honey-brown hair pulled back in a low ponytail. Honey-colored eyes. Piercings. Tattoos. A body with just the right amount of muscle and height." I sighed, trying hard not to drool as I remembered the image that was burned into my mind's eye.

"Who's that, hon?" Zoe Robinson set her Chardonnay down and leaned forward to fill her plate with wings, her caramel curls falling in front of her shoulders. Her fiancé, Chaz, took her four children to Matt and Tiffany's house to help out. And there was another great man. They were both lucky. "That description doesn't sound like any man from Mayflower." Her amber eyes looked at me curiously.

"Because he's not. His name is Byron Storm, and he went to college with Zander. The judge called in a favor and requested his old buddy to be my sponsor. Zander Jackson is trying to make me fail the program."

"Why do you say that?" Morticia Smith popped the top off a cola and poured some into a glass as she stared me down with intelligent dark eyes. Her long, silky black hair was secured in her usual knot at the back of her head.

"Because he knows exactly what my type looks like. There's no way I'm going to survive a 12-step program for sex addicts with a man like Byron Storm as my sponsor. How am I supposed to prove I don't have a problem, when the most delicious example of the male species I've ever seen is just a phone call away, ready to come help me with all of my needs?"

Thank God for my girls and ice-cold beer. We took turns hosting girls' night once a week at each other's houses to vent and support and cheer for each other through all of life's blessings and curses. Just like we had done back in high school.

"How have we never met this Byron Storm before?" Zoe bit into a slice of pizza and moaned in ecstasy. She had always been a foodie.

"Yeah, really. He sounds as yummy as this food." Tiff nibbled on a chicken wing then dabbed the corners of her mouth with a napkin.

"You haven't met him because he lives in Boston. Apparently, he went to BU with Zander. Most of the sponsors are sex addicts themselves who've successfully gone through the program. Byron is an actual mental health therapist who is certified in sex addiction because Zander claims I need *extra help*."

"I can't believe he is still bitter over you dumping him, doll. That was over twenty years ago." Tiffany shook her head.

"Right? I mean, let it go, dude." I grunted. "Since Mayflower is about an hour from the city, it probably wasn't much of a stretch to convince Byron to say yes. Plus, I heard him tell Shirley he owed Zander a favor. She wasn't too happy because I'm the only one who got a sponsor of the gender I was attracted to. She didn't want any unnecessary pressure put on us, but given his credentials, she agreed to the pairing."

"What are you going to do?" Morti sipped her cola.

"Whatever it takes. I have to make it through this program so the drama surrounding my life will stop. I don't even want a man anymore." I set my jaw with determination. "And you can bet I will damn sure find the person who started the crazy rumors that I'm a witch casting spells on men in the first place."

"Who do you think it could be?" Zoe looked pensive.

I shrugged. "Who knows. Maybe Phoenix Davenport."

"The new antique store owner?" Tiff asked.

"One and the same. It's a shame really. I thought with her green hair and nose ring, we might be friends, but no. She's had it out for me since the day she arrived."

"Why?" Morti asked.

"She doesn't like that I own a new age shop, yet I have

antique items in my store. If I find something cool, I add it to my shop. I don't care how old it is. I like alternative, different stuff. She told me to stay in my lane or else. Maybe she's trying to ruin my business, and this is her *or else.*"

"Whoever it is, we've got your back," Zoe said.

"And your front," Tiff added.

"And everything in between." Morti nodded. "Once we find the culprit, give me a shovel. I have the perfect place to dispose of the body."

"I love you babes." I blinked back tears.

I didn't show emotion often, but my girls got me every single time. Who needed a man when I had them? I would do anything for them, same as they would for me. And that was enough. Maybe I didn't need anything more...

Then why did my heart still feel like a piece of it was missing?

"Speaking of babes, are yours feeling any better, Tiff? Chaz told me about Genie's colic." Zoe winced. "I'm here to help if you ever need a break, hon."

The twins had been born early, but they'd been remarkably big and healthy and had gone home after a few days.

"Thanks, doll, I'm exhausted but Matt has actually been wonderful. Declan seems a little better, but Genie takes after Grammy. I have a feeling she's going to give me a lifetime of being difficult, but I wouldn't have it any other way." Tiffany hadn't even been sure she wanted children, yet she'd fallen in love with them instantly.

I secretly felt a little jealous, wishing my mother loved me just as fiercely. Then I immediately felt guilty. I was a grown ass woman. Forty, no less. I needed to let those feelings go once and for all, but for some reason I couldn't.

"Are you ready for your big day, Zoe?" I brought out a tub of ice cream with all the fixings to make sundaes. Dessert had always taken my mind off my troubles. "Anything else we can do to help?"

Zoe had wanted a small wedding. It was Chaz's first wedding, and the town adored him as well as his parents, but he just wanted Zoe. He didn't care about any other details, so Zoe was planning it her way. She refused to let anyone help with the planning because she was a party planner and wanted things done a certain way. But keeping up with the town's needs as well as her own was taking its toll.

"Yay." Tiffany clapped her hands. "We haven't had sundaes in so long." She grabbed a bowl and filled it as if she were still pregnant with twins.

Morti and I shot each other looks and grinned wide. Tiffany had been so concerned with looking perfect in the past. It was nice to see her with her walls down and just enjoying life for a change. Matt was good for her.

"I could not have done any of this without you girls." Zoe took a deep breath. "I just want everything to be perfect for Chaz. He has been such an amazing father to my children when their real dad couldn't care less about them. Lexi and Troy are old enough to remember and resent their dad, but Bobby and Katy were too young to really be hurt. Life as we know it is normal for them. Chaz is their knight in shining armor and my Prince Charming. I don't know what I would do without him."

"Me either. He's one amazing doctor." Tiffany nodded. "Dr. Joy might have delivered my twins, but Chaz has been their doctor since day one."

"He's my father's doctor, too." Morticia looked pensive. "Obviously with the whole doctor patient confidentiality, Chaz can't tell me anything. That doesn't mean I'm not overly curious about why my father has been seeing him so often lately."

"Is he sick?" Zoe looked at her with concern.

"No, he's healthy as a horse." Morti shrugged.

"Maybe I really am an addict because my mind went straight to Viagra." I looked at Morti. Her father's girlfriend was her age, or maybe even a little younger. "He'd better be using protection if he's using Viagra." Her face flushed beat red and not from embarrassment. She was fuming mad. Her mom died when she was so young, she never knew her. "It's always just been us. We are supposed to be a team. It should be my turn to move on to the next phase of marriage and children. I mean, I want him to be happy, but what about me, dammit? This had better just be a fling. If my own father has a baby before I do..." She just shook her head. "I sound like such a selfish bitch. Life is so damn hard sometimes."

"Tell me about it." My phone beeped with a text message.

Byron Storm here. Just checking in. Want to meet for coffee tomorrow morning?

Sure. Meet me at Pilgrim Perks Café at nine. My shop opens at ten.

I hit send with a shaking hand and realized life was about to get a whole lot harder.

Chapter Three

The next morning, I stood outside of *Pilgrim Perks Café*, shaking out my hands in hopes of shaking off my nerves before I walked through the front door. Byron Storm was in there waiting for me. We'd spoken briefly at the SAA meeting, but I didn't really know anything about him other than what I'd overheard.

"Come on, Harm, this is ridiculous. He's just a man." I grabbed the door and opened it more forcefully than necessary then marched inside. The aroma of fresh coffee and homemade baked goods doing little to calm my nerves.

Scanning the quaint café with bistro tables, a bar, and display of pastries, I found Byron sitting at a table in the corner. He was hard to miss. He wore tight fitting jeans, trendy shoes, and an eighties rock t-shirt that hugged his torso just the right amount to showcase his muscular body and the tattoos peeking out from beneath his short sleeves. He had a leather jacket draped over the back of his chair, and he'd left his hair down, the thick honey waves falling to his shoulders in glorious strands.

He glanced up and smiled, his warm honey eyes with gold flecks locking onto mine.

I swallowed hard. He wasn't just a man. He was a centerfold, for Bondye's sake.

I tried for a smile as I made my way over to his table and sat across from him. Slipping out of my jean jacket, I draped mine across the back of my chair and tried not to fidget in my skinny jeans and Looney Tunes t-shirt. I resisted the urge to touch my spiked hair. I'd added a little too much gel this morning, and my scalp itched.

"Hey," I said and sat on a chair.

"Hey, yourself," he responded and smiled.

I looked down at the black coffee in front of me. "How did you know my coffee order?" Was he a wizard? Maybe a warlock? Maybe a psychic? I blinked and peeked up at him, seeing him in a whole new light.

I frowned.

Or maybe he was just *psycho.*

He chuckled. "I can see the wheels in your head spinning into overdrive, Harmony." His voice was soft and warm like melted taffy from Willy Wonka's factory.

My lips parted over hearing him speak my first name.

"Zander told me your coffee order," he explained his wizardry. "He said it was what you drank in high school and that you're just as bold now as you were back then, so he didn't figure you'd changed much."

"Well, he figured wrong, Mr. Storm." I lied and added

cream and sugar then took a big sip and struggled not to gag.

Byron's eyes twinkled with merriment, but he wisely kept the smirk off his face. "Please, call me Byron."

"I don't even know you."

"And that's the point." He took a sip of his steaming black coffee, and I looked on enviously.

Damn my stubborn pride. Defiantly, I took another sip of my sweet concoction, hoping it would grow on me. It didn't. I glanced up and caught him studying me.

"If I'm going to be your sponsor, you need to get comfortable enough with me to tell me anything."

"Fine, I like my coffee black," I admitted, then thrust a finger in his direction, "but that doesn't mean Zander knows me or that I haven't changed."

"Fair enough." Byron signaled the waiter for a refill.

Rose Theodore stuck her nose in the air when she walked past us, making a beeline for the door. She was the town's librarian and didn't like that I sold books of any kind in my shop, let alone ones that should be banned in her eyes.

"Who was that?" He pushed his cup to the edge of the table for the waiter to refill with black coffee.

"An old rival." I sighed before asking the waiter for a new cup. "So, how does this work? I thought I would only see you if I called you for help?"

"Normally, yes, but Zander thinks you need *extra* help."

"Oh, he does, does he?" I narrowed my eyes. "Trust

me, Zander doesn't know a thing about meeting my needs." I stifled a snort, remembering that one time back in high school, and tried not to shudder.

That wasn't why I broke up with him.

Zander went around bragging about how good he was in bed and sharing intimate details with the football team. I was mortified. He'd really hurt my feelings, and he'd never once apologized for that. I could have shared how terrible he was at sex back then, but I didn't. I'd simply broken up with him and moved on. Or tried to, but no guy took me seriously after that. They only wanted one thing. Now the tables had turned, and I couldn't even get a guy to give me a second look.

Zander was loving every minute of it.

Byron studied me with patient, understanding, warm brown eyes. "I can see that Zander is a touchy subject for you."

I shrugged. "Let's just say Zander would have preferred I choose jail, but my mother has a way of getting what she wants."

"I'm guessing SAA?"

"Exactly." I set my jaw. "I know you probably won't believe me, but I'm really not a sex addict."

He remained calm and unbiased. "It's not about what I believe."

"It is to me." I swallowed past the lump in my throat. I hated showing any vulnerability, especially with seven older brothers.

"Then tell me your side," he said without missing a beat.

"It's hard not to be a tomboy growing up in my family, and yes, I can come on a little strong sometimes, but I have never crossed a line. Someone started spreading rumors that I am a witch who casts spells to force men to go out with me, and now everyone is running scared. I'm really *not* that scary."

His lips tipped up slightly at the corners. "You don't look scary to me."

I blinked. "I don't?" I shook off the urge to ask him out. What was wrong with me? He was my sponsor. "I mean, I know, right? I don't, and I'm not. Don't get me wrong, I like sex, but I'm far from an addict." I felt my cheeks flush. "I'm lonely. I just want someone to share my life with. A companion."

"Completely understandable." His voice softened, and his eyes filled with compassion. "We all want to feel loved."

"Exactly." He was such a good listener. My gaze locked onto his, drawn to him more than any man I'd met in a long time, but I couldn't have him no matter how much I might want him. I sighed and nodded. "Even if I'm not guilty, my sentence is to successfully complete this 12-step program when Dr. Hastings says so."

"Then that's what you'll do." He nodded.

I was already shaking my head. "I'm not so sure now. I have a feeling Zander is setting me up to fail."

Byron squinted. "Why do you say that?"

"Because he pulled some strings to make a man like *you* be my sponsor."

He arched a brow high. "And that is a problem because...?"

Whoops. "It's not a problem. I just mean you're an actual therapist. A little overqualified if you ask me. Why would you agree to be my sponsor?"

He hesitated a moment. "Let's just say I owe Zander a favor from a long time ago, and this will finally make us even." He didn't go into further detail, and I had a feeling he wouldn't. He seemed closed off on that topic, so I changed it.

"But you live in Boston. How is this going to work?"

"I rented Quincy Cottage on Freedom Lake for however long it takes you to get through the program."

"But what about your clients?"

"Telehealth." He took a sip of steaming black coffee. "I work mostly from home these days anyway."

"Well..."

"You're running out of excuses as to why I can't be your sponsor, Harmony." He stared me down with suspicious eyes.

I cleared my throat, unable to admit the real reason why I didn't want him as my sponsor. "I guess that settles it then. So, what's next, Big Brother?"

"Wrong program." He chuckled.

"You know what I mean. What do I call you, anyway?"

"Byron will do." He smiled a genuine, kind smile. The kind that makes a person believe every word that comes out of his mouth. I literally would jump off the Millenium Falcon if he told me to. "As for how this works, you'll start the program. You go to group as often as you need to. We hang out and get to know each other better. I give you the extra help the judge ordered. And you call me day or night any time you need me. Sound good?"

"Sure," I said weakly, thinking, this didn't sound good at all. This sounded very bad because something told me Mr. Byron Storm would know exactly how to meet my needs...and then some.

A couple days later, I sat at a table in McGinny's Pub with my girls for a much-needed night out. Tiffany's fiancé, Matt, came straight from Ireland to take over the pub from his uncle. He was even bigger than my brothers and father, which I hadn't thought possible until I met the McGinnis clan. Big, strapping, curly golden-blond-haired, blue-eyed Irishmen with hearty laughs and welcoming personalities.

"What can I get ye lasses?" Matt flashed his deep dimples at us, revealing perfectly straight white teeth.

"A beer for me." I took off my coat.

"Chardonnay for me." Zoe smiled her thanks.

"Diet cola for me." Morti nodded.

"Better make mine sparkling water, doll." Tiff sighed. "I could fall asleep right now, and we've barely just arrived."

"Ye can have one, love. Yer mammy and sister can

handle the twins for a wee bit longer." Matt got busy pouring our drinks.

"Speaking of the wee ones," Chaz said with his whiskey-smooth voice, "I'd better get home to ours." His sandy hair was Ken doll perfect, and his hazel eyes were filled with love as he leaned down and kissed Zoe's cheek after dropping her off.

"Thanks, hon." She gave him a hug before he left.

"You both are so lucky." Morti sighed, looking around the pub. "I just wish I could find a good man like that."

"You're not going to find him in a book, doll," Tiffany said gently.

"No, but in my online book club I might. It would be nice to find someone with common interests."

"Dude, I would be happy to find someone at all." I frowned, feeling anger rise inside of me once more over the injustice of it all. "I need to find who started the rumors about me in the first place."

"Do you have any idea?" Zoe sipped her Chardonnay.

"Not a clue. I mean, it could have been someone I dated in the past. Several of those relationships ended badly. Or a jealous ex-girlfriend of one of the guys. It could be someone who doesn't like my shop. This town is so old-fashioned. It could be our resident busy bodies, Gerty and Gabby Rogers. We all know how they love to stir up drama. All I know is that once I'm out of this program, the rumors need to end so I can get on with my life."

"I agree." Tiff sipped the Champagne Matt had brought her with a moan of pleasure. "Oh, how I missed this, but my tolerance sure isn't what it used to be. I can already feel just this one glass going straight to my head, and we all know that's how I got into trouble the first time."

"Speaking of trouble." Morti looked at the door.

Zander walked into the pub, out of his judge's robes, wearing khakis and an olive-green sweater. He was a tall, dark, and handsome force to be reckoned with. Too bad his personality wasn't nearly as attractive.

"Just great." I groaned, and then sucked in a sharp breath when a second man entered right behind him.

"Wow, who's that?" Zoe gaped with her mouth open.

"That is my sponsor, Byron Storm."

"Oh, doll, you were right. You are most definitely in trouble." Tiffany watched them take a table not too far from ours.

"Right? How am I supposed to stick to the program with him around?" Just the sight of him stirred something deep inside of me, more than just the physical, and that was the part that scared me most of all.

As if there were some magnetic force between us, Byron's eyes met mine. He smiled slowly and sent me a nod.

"Oh, yeah, you've got it bad." Morti raised a black brow at me and then glanced back at Byron. "And from the look on his face when you weren't watching, I'd say he feels the same way. That's double trouble if you ask me."

"You're crazy." I studied Byron more curiously now, but whatever expression Morti thought she saw was gone.

"He's a therapist and my sponsor. He doesn't feel anything out of the ordinary for me."

"I'm with Morti, doll. I saw his expression, too, and I know when a man's interested," Tiffany agreed. "You two have serious chemistry. He's all man, and you're one hot woman. Maybe he's the man you've been looking for."

I was already shaking my head. "He might be, but there's no sex allowed while in the program." My gaze kept getting drawn to his. "It's against the rules."

"Wasn't it you who once told me rules were meant to be broken?" Zoe raised her glass to me. "His tattoos and ponytail tell me he might be open to breaking a rule or two. You've been searching for a man like him since forever. You never know if there is anything there unless you try. He's going to be spending a lot of time with you, after all."

Morti snapped her fingers. "I know where I've seen him. He's staying at Quincy Cottage right down from our funeral home."

"He sure is." I nodded and swallowed hard. "I'm not looking for anything serious, and I don't want to get hurt. Not to mention he doesn't even live in Mayflower. His whole life is in Boston."

"Which isn't that far away. This could still work." Zoe was always the practical one of the group. The voice of reason. But also, the hopeless romantic. "We just want you to be happy, Harm. You don't have to prove anything to anyone. There's nothing wrong with you, and you didn't break the law. Go through the program because *Zander* is making you, but don't miss out on something that could be amazing."

"I don't need sex to be happy." Getting turned down by the men in Mayflower sucked, but I didn't think I could handle getting turned down by a man like Byron Storm. "All I want is companionship. It will be nice to have someone to spend time with. Someone to go to all the town events with. A sort of date to make my mother happy. And the best part is I won't be lonely. Sounds like a win-win to me. I'm beginning to think sex is overrated."

"If you say so." Morti snorted. "I'm rooting for you, Harm, but I've got twenty bucks that says you can't be just friends with a man like Byron. Hell, I don't think any of us could or would even want to. Zander is just being petty and trying to get even with you."

"I'm with Morti, doll." Tiff lifted her hands up. "We all know you're not a sex addict, but as your best friends, we also know it's been a very long time. Overrated or not, I don't think you will be able to abstain for long with Studmuffin Storm around, and you did all bet on me recently. So, count me in."

"Well, shoot, I guess I'm in too. Sorry, Harm. I know what it was like when Max left. It was two years of me abstaining from sex, so there was no way I could resist Chaz. If there is nothing between you and Byron and you end up just being friends, then I'll gladly shell over my twenty. Get through the program, but I'm secretly hoping Byron turns out to be the best birthday present you've ever received because we love you. You deserve the best, hon."

Zander's gaze trailed over to mine, and a knowing smirk crossed his face. I knew what he was thinking. How does it feel to want something you can't have? Payback's a bitch, babe. He gave me a little wave, and the strongest urge to punch him swept over me. I wasn't a violent person by nature, more of a lover than a fighter, but I was raised to stand up for myself. The honorable Zander Jackass was playing games with me, and I didn't like it one bit.

I also didn't like to lose...

"You're on, ladies," I said without taking my eyes off Zander, "and I intend to win."

Chapter Four

It was the first week of February. My birthday month was officially over, thank God. A fresh start with my new *friend*.

"You ready?" I came to a stop outside of Quincy Cottage, got out of my car, ran around the hood, and then opened the passenger side door to my rusted tie-died Love Bug. "Your chariot awaits." I grinned wide.

"That's one word for it." Byron chuckled as he slid into the vehicle and closed the creaky door after him.

I jogged around the front and slid into the driver's side, closing my own squeaky door. "Cheyenne was a chariot back in her day."

"She has character, I'll give her that..." he looked down, and his eyebrows crept higher, "...and holes in her floor."

"She can be a little trashy, but she's a good girl." I winked as I put her into drive. "My brother Homer, who's the youngest of the boys, owns a body shop. He's the best mechanic around these parts, but he's obsessed with fixing up his prized Mustang. Been promising me for months he would patch her up. At this point, I'm ready to do it myself."

"I'm pretty handy with cars." Byron shrugged. "I could help you out if you want since I'll be in town for a while."

"I just might take you up on that." I drove down Lighthouse Lane until I came to *Colonial Cuts* and pulled into the parking lot.

"Why are we here at a barber shop?" He studied me curiously.

I tried not to fidget. "You asked me where I got my hair cut."

He blinked. "I assumed you went to a salon."

I gave him a flat look. "You assumed wrong."

He held his hands up. "Okay, then. My bad."

I sighed. "Sorry. I'm just sick of my mother trying to make me more girly, and everyone else misunderstanding me in general."

"Got it."

"She goes to *Timeless Tresses* but trust me when I say you want *Colonial Cuts*. I started going with my father and brothers when I was little. My mother has tried to convert me to a salon for years, but I won't let anyone touch my hair except RJ. Besides, the salon charges astronomical prices compared to the barbershop."

"True, but I've always found you get what you pay for."

"It's true that some barbers are only good with clippers, but RJ is a wizard with a pair of scissors and clippers. He can do it all." I peeked over at Byron before I shut the car off and couldn't help but tease him a little. "We can go to the salon if the barbershop is too manly for you."

"Very funny." He looked up at the barbershop pole mounted on the exterior of the shop near the entrance. "*Colonial Cuts* it is."

Mayflower might be old fashioned, which drove me crazy at times, but I did like how she kept some historical traditions alive. A traditional barbershop pole stood at the edge of the sidewalk just outside the door. The tall, cylinder glass shape with red, white, and blue spiraling stripes rotating inside had remained an icon for years. It even had a light at the top and the bottom, making it easy to identify what type of shop it was.

"Did you know," I began, to break what I felt was the beginning of an awkward sentence. "Originally, in the Middle Ages, barbers cut hair, extracted teeth, and performed minor surgeries. The red and white stripes signified historical bloodletting and bandages, and the pole represented the staff patients would grip to make their veins bulge to make bloodletting easier." I watched Byron's brows creep toward his hairline. "The blue stripe was a later addition."

"Fascinating," he said on a wispy breath, like he'd learned something new and really cared about it.

"Right?" I exclaimed rather loudly because I wasn't too

sure about that weird flip in my stomach and needed to break the spell.

Then again, I found a lot of things fascinating, including my sponsor. Part of what had gotten me in trouble in the first place. I shut off the engine and led the way inside. All eyes turned in our direction. A couple men got up and left, giving me a wide berth on their way out. I rolled my eyes. There were three barber chairs in use.

One barber, named Norman, was in his eighties with a full head of gray curls. He refused to retire because he loved his job. He was giving our mail carrier, old man Truman Winters, a hot shave. The other barber, Sylvester aka Sly, was barely out of high school but great with the latest trends. He sported a purple faded buzzcut and a lip ring as he worked his magic on creating a teenage boy's new style. And then there was the barbershop owner, Rupert Junior aka RJ. He was around fifty and didn't have a lick of hair.

"I'll be with you in a minute, Harmony." RJ waved his scissors around as he talked. "Running a little behind because Mack here was late.

"Sorry, Miss Jones." Mack shot me an apologetic look and shrugged. "I was supposed to have the day off, but I went in to help a little this morning. That last winter storm was a doozy. We're still cleaning up the woods of the destruction it did to some of the older trees. Old age affects us all."

"Ain't that the truth." Old man Winters rubbed his knees. "Gonna be another storm soon. Mark my words."

Truman's knees never lied. I chewed my bottom lip. "Is my father still out there?"

"You know your pa. Arnold puts in more time than all of us together, yet he's a good ten or twenty years older than most of us. He's one tough jack." Mack was almost as big as my father but not quite, and around sixty.

My father was seventy, but he also refused to retire.

I smiled at Mack, hiding my worry about my father still being in the woods with a storm on the way. "Take your time, RJ. I can hold off on a trim for myself, so I'm giving my spot to my friend here, Byron Storm." I jerked my head in Byron's direction.

"Nice to meet you, Byron. Have a seat, and I'll be with you shortly." RJ nodded and went back to trimming Mack's salt and pepper hair and beard.

"Jack?" Byron asked, keeping his voice low.

"Mack and my father are lumberjacks. They work in the logging industry, cutting, processing, and transporting trees for manufacturing and production."

"That seems like rough work for men that age." Byron did a double take in Mack's direction, not that he could see too much with the barber's cape draped over him.

"It is." I snagged two mints from a dish near RJ's station and handed one to Byron. "They've worked together for years felling trees, removing branches, cutting trees into logs, skidding them, and loading the logs onto trucks which transport them to sawmills."

"This is done year round? It seems as if it could be so unforgiving."

"Well," I continued, "it can be if careless mistakes are made, which is why my father and Mack work so well together. Winter presents challenges for sure, but frozen ground sometimes makes transporting heavy logs easier with less damage to the forest floor." I paused briefly, surprised he remained glued to what I was saying. "In the off-season, they maintain their equipment, help train new jacks in safety measures, and they've even been involved in sustainable practices like reforestation."

"Incredible. I guess I never realized people still do this kind of thing. I always thought of it as a lost art." Byron stared at me with an intense fascination I'd only seen from my best friends who completely understood my passions.

I led the way towards the back of the room near the game table. Al Shanker and Walter Wimbledon were playing checkers. They both were in their forties and businessmen. Al owned *Shanker's Smoke Shop* on the edge of town and Walter owned *Walt's Single Malts* liquor store right across the street from my shop on Lighthouse Lane. They were talking with their heads bent together and hadn't seen us yet.

"Do you think the rumors are true?" Al asked, making a move forward with his single red checker on the checkerboard. Al was a short man, maybe five-foot-five, with thinning brown hair and a slight stature.

"I heard she sacrifices animals and drinks their blood." Walter shuddered, his chubby cheeks jiggling as he moved his single black checker to block Al's red one.

"That would explain the decapitated mouse poor Peter

found on his front porch." Al shook his head, his scalp showing through his deep widow's peak. He made a countermove with his red checker.

"I don't know if he'll ever be the same." Walter tsked, moving his black checker in another direction, neither man making progress.

"Oh, how awful." I stood over their hunched bodies. "I can't imagine who would do such a thing. Can you?" I crossed my arms, towering over them both with my feet planted firmly apart, daring them to accuse me directly.

Al shook his head no, his gaze shifting between Byron and me. "Just repeating what we heard."

"Nothing good ever came from spreading rumors." Byron set his jaw. "Especially when they're untrue."

"Don't worry, gentlemen." I kept my face blank as I said, "I will call upon the spirits tonight at my altar and ask for help."

Byron stifled a groan and shook his head.

I couldn't help myself.

"S-Spirits?" Walter swallowed hard.

"W-What kind?" Al gaped.

"Don't you boys worry. I have the perfect ritual in mind. I'll fix poor Peter up good." I winked.

Queen me, bitches!

The men looked at each other, got up, and promptly left the barbershop.

Byron sighed. "You know that's just going to fuel the rumors even more."

"I don't care. Ignorant people infuriate me." Maybe it was time I did something about it.

"Here, let me help you." I grabbed several shopping bags from the back of my car while Byron carried the takeout later that evening.

"Thanks. Guess I bought more than I realized." He led the way inside Quincy Cottage and set the takeout on the island while I set the packages on the kitchen table.

I'd dragged him all over town, trying to figure out who was responsible for starting the rumors about me without much luck, while he gave me advice on how to handle various situations so I didn't get myself into any more trouble. I had to admit we made a pretty good team. People in Mayflower might like to gossip, but they also loved a good secret. Even if they knew who the culprit was, they would never tell.

They lived for the drama.

"My mother would love you. I hate to shop." I gestured toward the numerous bags full of items he had purchased.

"Those aren't for me."

"Oh, I see," was all I said. I'd never given thought that he might have someone special waiting for him back in Boston. Although, he was gorgeous, so of course he would. He was only in Mayflower for work, after all, and because he owed Zander a favor.

"I have two sisters, three nieces, and my mother back in

Boston who will have something to say if I don't bring them back presents." He chuckled softly, and I caught him staring at me curiously.

Damn my open-book face.

"Oh, okay, good," I said a lot more upbeat. "I mean, that's sweet of you to think of your family." This time I studied him. "I noticed you only shopped at the small businesses, and not any of the chain stores."

"What can I say?" He shrugged, his eyes never leaving mine. "I have a soft spot for the underdog." He was always studying me, analyzing me. I knew it wasn't in a romantic way. It couldn't be. He was just being thorough, doing his job.

I needed to remember that.

My heart did a funny little flip anyway. "So, it would seem." I cleared my throat. "I should get going. Truman was right. It's snowing like crazy. I should have expected that. We get lake effect snow a lot."

He looked at me from where he stood in the kitchen. "I've noticed that. We can get intense weather like a blizzard or hurricane in Boston because of the ocean, but this lake effect stuff off Freedom Lake is crazy."

I looked out the window at the lake and couldn't see anything. Wind blew big, fat flakes around creating white-out conditions.

"Great. Looks like I'm not going anywhere anytime soon. That's going to get tongues wagging for sure since my car's pretty hard to miss. People are going to know if I spend the night here." Darn Truman for always being right. And here I had been worried about my father, except he wasn't the one in trouble.

I was.

Suddenly the power went out.

"Well, you might not have a choice. Don't worry so much about what people think. I'm your sponsor. I'm supposed to be helping you cope with everyday stressors." The sun had already set, so the cottage had plunged into total darkness. Byron turned on his cell phone flashlight. "Don't worry. There's a wood fireplace, fully stocked and ready to go. I got it ready the other day but haven't had a chance to use it yet."

"Dude, you're a lifesaver. I'm freezing." I followed his light.

He chuckled. "Rolling around in the snow will do that to you."

"It was slippery. I couldn't get up." I pleaded my case from my earlier debacle. The snow had fallen so quickly, the roads and sidewalks were a mess. I'd fallen flat on my backside and couldn't get up for several moments.

"I tried to help, but someone wouldn't let me." He performed the sexiest brow arch I'd ever seen.

"Hey, I was doing you a favor by not bringing you down with me." I fought not to stutter, whether from the cold or my nerves, I wasn't sure. "No sense in both of us getting soaked. My mother always tells me I never dress correctly for the season. I should have worn boots instead of sneakers, just in case, but the weather channel hadn't predicted the storm. From now on I'm going straight to the only accurate source...Weatherman Winters."

"He does seem to know what he's talking about. Let me get this fire started, then I'll find you something to wear."

I ignored my chattering teeth, not having realized just how soaked I was until everything melted. It wasn't long before a roaring fire blasted heat into the small cottage. Byron disappeared down the hall towards the bedrooms, emerging moments later.

"I put a sweatsuit and thick socks on the bed in the guest bedroom. They'll be big on you, but they should be warm."

"Oh, my God, you're the best, babe."

Byron paused a beat, his forehead crinkling.

"What?" I asked.

"Babe?" he questioned.

I waved my hand dismissively. "Oh, that. I call everyone babe. Force of habit. Nothing more."

"Okay." He let it go. "I just don't want to do anything to set you back in your progress in the program."

Now it was my turn to pause. "You really think I'm a sex addict, don't you?" His answer shouldn't mean anything to me, but it did. After spending the day together, I actually cared what he thought.

"It's not my place to judge. I'm only here to support you on your journey and help you navigate temptations."

"Careful, *babe*, I might jump your bones when I get back." I jogged off to the bedroom with my cell phone flashlight guiding my way. Peeling off my wet clothes, I slid into Byron's soft, charcoal gray sweatsuit and thick socks, feeling better instantly.

"Why do you do that?" Byron studied me with those warm, honey-brown, all-seeing eyes when I joined him in the living room.

I sat down on the other end of the couch and picked up the beer he'd opened for me, taking a swig before I spoke. "Do what?" I knew what he meant, but shrugging things off and putting on a front was second nature to me.

I'd been doing it my whole life.

He took a swig of his own beer then leaned back and crossed his feet on the coffee table as if taking a minute to ponder his own words. "When confronted with a challenging situation, you respond with humor and sarcasm, often going for shock and awe."

I shrugged. "You tell me, Doc. Why do *you* think I do that?"

"I think you're deflecting," he said without missing a beat this time.

I frowned. "Deflecting what?" This was getting a bit too real, and I wasn't sure how I felt about having a therapy session right now.

His voice gentled. "You don't want people to see how you really feel."

"Yeah? And how's that?" I tried to stay casual, nonchalant, but it was difficult not to get defensive.

"Hurt. Unaccepted." His eyes met mine. "Unlovable."

I blinked and swallowed hard, remaining silent. How could he possibly know me so well already?

"You don't have to be so tough, Harm. It's okay to be vulnerable. You're so afraid if people get to know the real you, they won't love you for who you are. So, you hide by being tough, a little over the top, a little outrageous. Then if people reject you, they're rejecting your persona and not you. Because if they reject the real you, then it means you're not good enough. You're a failure." He paused until I looked at him. "You let your mother down."

"My mother?" I breathed in awe. My biggest fear had always been in letting my mother down. How could he possibly know that?

"You put far too much pressure on yourself over being the only daughter, Harmony. You're the one who is sabotaging yourself."

My jaw unhinged. "You don't know what you're talking about."

"I have a couple degrees that say I do." He shrugged one shoulder and took another sip of his beer. "You asked for my honest opinion, and I gave it. You don't have to like it, but you do have to accept it. What you choose to do with it is up to you."

Well, hell.

I didn't know what to say. What to do. I downed the rest of my beer. "Well, thanks for letting me crash here, given the weather and power outage. It's been a hell of a day. Think I'll go to bed."

His gaze locked onto mine. "Yeah, it's getting late. Think I'll go to bed, too."

Another intense moment lingered between us, before I surged to my feet and headed down the hall without looking back, closing the guest bedroom door firmly behind me.

He'd touched on so many things I'd never told anyone, not even my best friends. He'd said what I chose to do with it was up to me...

Frankly, I didn't have a clue.

Chapter Five

"I can't believe I'm here." I groaned the next day after a restless night of no sleep.

I'd slipped out before Byron had even awakened, leaving him a note of thanks. Today was a new day, and I needed to remain focused. No distractions. I walked into *Mayflower Community Center* where the Bedazzled Boomers group was meeting.

I swore I would never attend a meeting that had the word *bedazzled* in it. I didn't want to give my mother false hope, but I didn't have a choice. The only way Peter Sherman would meet with me was through a supervised visit. He wanted a safe space with support, so we'd chosen the Bedazzled Boomers with both our mothers present.

SAA meetings were held daily, but attendance wasn't mandatory. You went whenever you felt the need. So, I'd attended a second meeting without Byron, hoping for a little more clarity. A few people popped in and out, but it was pretty much the same six people, so we unofficially formed our own little support group. The program required that I first admit I was powerless over sex and that my life had become unmanageable.

Yes, my life had become unmanageable, but it was because I *wasn't* having sex.

A higher power was supposed to restore me to sanity. Even though my family was Catholic, I didn't worship a specific god, goddess, or supreme being. I focused on the power of nature, the universe, and my own inner strength. I was supposed to turn my will and my life over to this being as I know him, and then take a moral inventory of myself.

Admittedly, there were several things I could improve upon.

I was supposed to admit these things to Byron and ask my higher power to remove my shortcomings. Not ready to see the all-knowing Byron after he'd already pointed out some of my shortcomings, I skipped ahead in the steps. I made a list of all the people I had supposedly wronged. According to the police report, that was half the town, with Peter Sherman right at the top.

I sighed. This was going to take a while.

Making amends with good ole PeeWee was the first step.

"Oh, Harmony, I'm so glad you're here." My mother, Wanda, hurried over to me, her pale green eyes so like mine, sparkling with delight. She smoothed back her shoulder-length, light-brown hair, which was already styled to perfection, as she stood much shorter than me. She spun around, showing off the Valentine's Day vest she had bedazzled as it hugged her curves. The light reflected off the sparkling jewels. "Isn't this grand?" She blinked up at me with a face full of artfully applied makeup.

My mother didn't even go to the mailbox without her face on and hair styled.

"Very nice, Mom." I smiled, wanting to please her. She never came right out and said I didn't please her, but I could tell I was a disappointment as her only daughter.

I wasn't anything like her.

She peeked past me. "Where's your handsome young fellow?"

"Byron isn't my fellow. He's my sponsor."

"Sponsor, companion...same difference." She grinned wide. "So, when are you going to see him again?"

So *not* the same difference.

He was supposed to keep me from having sex, not be a willing participant, but there was no talking to my mother. She had a one-track mind and tunnel vision when it came to my love life.

I took a deep breath and strove for patience. "I'm sure I will see him soon. Right now, I need to keep progressing through this program."

"Okay, dear, but don't keep him waiting too long. Men don't like that. You don't want him to grow bored with you and jump off the hook since it took so long for you to catch him. I don't think there are plenty of fish in *your* sea, dear."

She patted my arm and then pulled me across the room when she spotted Beverly Sherman waving at us.

Beverly was tall and thin, just like Peter, with dark brown hair and glasses. She clapped her hands excitedly when we reached her. No wonder they were such good friends. They were just alike. She proudly wore a vest very similar to my mother's, spinning about in an exuberant twirl. "Aren't these vests to die for?"

"I know. I just love mine. We can help you make one if you'd like, dear." My mother blinked up at me with high expectations shining in her eyes. "Heather here is a wiz at bedazzling. She bedazzled all her own outfits for the Miss Mayflower pageant. I'm sure she would love to help you, wouldn't you, dear?"

Heather appeared from behind my mother, her beaming smile slipping when she saw me. "Harmony doesn't seem like the sparkly type, but of course, I'm always up for helping those less fortunate."

I ground my teeth, but kept my smile firmly pasted in place. "Maybe later." I forced a look of disappointment and tapped my watch. "Unfortunately, I'm short on time."

My mother's face lost some of its sparkle, but then her eyes lit up as she looked around. "We have a good turnout tonight. Even the mayor's wife, Eleanor, is here. She's sitting with Gerty and Gabby Rogers, of course."

"Of course, she is." Beverly rolled her eyes. "Even if she didn't want to sit with them, she wouldn't have a choice with those two. Eleanor is way too classy of a lady and far too nice to say anything."

"Speaking of new people, where is Peter?" I asked Beverly.

"Peter's coming?" Heather's face brightened.

"Yes, to see *me*, but don't worry. He won't need your help. He's not very sparkly, either." I fluttered my lashes at her.

She narrowed her eyes and went back to the table with the other Bedazzlers.

"Oh, he'll be here in a minute," Beverly went on, oblivious to Heather's crush on her son. "He's a bit shy."

"Really?" That was one word for it.

"I still have hope you two can work things out." Beverly giggled.

Not likely.

"Oh, no, my Harmony has a new man. Maybe you've seen him around?" My mother beamed a proud smile at me.

"Well, now that you mention it, I have."

"He's not my—"

"Oh, look, here's Peter now." Beverly flagged Peter down.

Peter slowly walked over to us, stopping a good six feet from me. "Mother. Mrs. Jones. You ladies are looking splendiferous this fine evening." He didn't acknowledge if he'd even seen me, when I knew damn well he had.

"Why, aren't you just the cat's meow." My mother blushed.

"Oh, Petey, you're such a charmer." His mother giggled again.

I struggled not to roll my eyes. "I'm just dandy, in case you're wondering, *Petey*, and how are you?"

He finally looked at me with disgust, his cheeks growing pink. "Still waiting for an apology, Miss Jones...or should I say witch?"

"I didn't do anything wrong. I simply tried to set the mood and call on a little help in the romance department, because let's face it...we both needed it. You're the one who went shrieking out of my apartment like a fox during mating season without the pleasure of mating. I'll pass, thank you very much."

"Trust me, I wasn't offering," he said dryly.

"Trust me, I'm no longer that desperate," I ground out through my clenched teeth.

He shook his head. "Why am I here?"

I groaned with the thought of what I had to do no matter how much it killed me. I bit my tongue and inhaled a huge breath. "To make amends."

"How, by insulting me?"

"I'm sorry you misinterpreted the situation."

"What a backhanded apology. That is not taking ownership for your actions and admitting you harmed me. You're not sorry one bit."

"You're right, because I didn't do anything wrong!" I blurted, drawing all eyes to us, regretting my words and my stubborn pride immediately.

"Then there's nothing more to say." He turned around and marched across the room and out the door.

"Bye, Peter." Heather gloated.

"Oh, my." Beverly swooned.

"Oh, dear." My mother pouted.

Oh, hell, I thought. I would never graduate from the SAA program at this rate. I was tempted to break into jail and be done with it.

"I can't believe your big day is finally here, babe." I hugged Zoe tightly.

"You look stunning, doll." Tiffany hugged her next.

"I'm digging our deep red dresses. Nice choice for a Valentine's Day wedding, Zoe." Morticia hugged her last. "Then again, everything you plan is always amazing."

"Thanks, hon. I couldn't have done any of this without you ladies supporting me every step of the way. I love you all so much."

Zoe and Chaz had chosen to have a small wedding inside their huge, gorgeous house. Her parents, Wilma and Robert Fitzgerald, and her former in-laws, Lilabelle and Johnboy Robinson, as well as Chaz's parents, Roz and Wally Anderson, were all in attendance. They didn't always get along with each other, but they all adored Zoe, her children, and Chaz.

Tiffany, Morticia, and I were bridesmaids. Zoe's daughter, Lexi, was the maid of honor, and her youngest daughter, Katy, was the flower girl. Chaz's father was his best man, and Zoe's youngest son, Bobby, was the ring bearer.

Tiffany's fiancé, Matt, was a groomsman and walking with her, while Morticia was walking with Zoe's older son, Troy. They'd paired me up with Chaz's friend from college, Jinwoo Park, and I didn't mind one bit.

He didn't know a thing about me or the stupid rumors.

Originally from Korea, Jinwoo had studied abroad and met Chaz in grad school in Boston. He loved the United States so much, he got a job in the tech industry in Seattle, and they'd never lost touch.

I brought Byron as my plus one because I felt bad leaving him alone at the cottage, and well, he was in town to support me, after all. People would expect to see him with me so I wouldn't fall off the wagon, so to speak, even though I had no intention of climbing onto anyone's wagon.

I had a program to get through, a point to prove, and a bet to win.

Truthfully, I wasn't succeeding that well on my own. My attempt to apologize to Peter was proof of that. I'd been avoiding Byron ever since the storm, but clearly, I needed his help. I wasn't avoiding him because I was worried about anything romantic happening between us, no matter what the girls thought.

They were crazy.

Byron was nothing but professional and always a gentleman. I was mostly avoiding him because he made me feel vulnerable when he was around. He could see right through all my defenses and read me too well. It made me feel naked. Exposed.

For once, I didn't like that.

"It's time," Tiffany said, snapping me out of my thoughts.

The music started downstairs, and the hum of conversation ceased. It was an evening wedding. Candles glowed softly, filling the room along with red, pink, and white roses. It looked elegant and beautiful, just like Zoe.

Tiff and Matt slowly made their way down the long, winding staircase to stand on the sides of the makeshift altar in the great room in front of a crackling fireplace. Next, Morti and Troy followed suit. Jinwoo held out his arm and gave me a dazzling smile. I slid my arm through his and stifled a frown when a whisper trickled through my brain, secretly wishing the arm belonged to a certain therapist.

What was wrong with me?

Halfway down the stairs, I knew exactly what was wrong with me. I was hot for the teacher...or in this case, the sponsor. I sighed, tearing my gaze away from the honey-brown eyes that were always watching me. I hated that he knew exactly what I was thinking at any given moment, yet I couldn't read him at all.

Did he care that I was holding onto another man?

Did I want him to?

I shook off that train of thought, knowing it would only lead to trouble.

Pasting a smile on my face, I looked around at all the guests sitting in rows of chairs. The Andersons were highly respected and knew a ton of people, but Zoe and Chaz only invited their closest friends and family. My gaze locked onto my mother's beaming one, and I gave her a head nod. Doing the same to my father, brothers, sisters-in-law, and nephews, I took my place beside the girls and tried not to look at who was officiating.

Judge Jackson.

Zoe had a large Catholic wedding the first time around. This time she wanted a small, intimate ceremony, and Chaz was on board with anything that made her happy. Just because I had a problem with Zander didn't mean the others did. We all went to high school together, and he was the only judge in town. Zoe didn't want any of her friends and family to get ordained so they could offici-ate. She wanted them to attend the wedding and be present, so Judge Zander was the logical choice and happy to comply...

And watch me like a hawk in the process.

The ceremony began, only lasting about twenty minutes. Even I had to admit Zander did a great job. There wasn't a dry eye in the room. Touching, sweet, funny... everything Zoe wanted. And now the reception had started.

Zoe and Chaz took to the dance floor, and the rest of the wedding party followed suit.

"So, how long have you known Zoe?" Jinwoo led me around the dance floor in a perfect waltz.

I smiled up at him, ignoring the fact that Byron and Zander were deep in conversation. "My whole life. I know you know the Doctor Chaz from college, but we went to school together. Actually, the five of us did. Chaz was four years younger than us and a lot shyer back then, but he always had a thing for Zoe."

"I can see why. She's a great lady." His gaze locked onto mine. "You all are."

Oh, yeah. He definitely had not heard the rumors.

"Thanks, babe." *Shoot.* I really needed to stop doing that.

His lips tipped up at the corners.

"Sorry if that's weird. Force of habit. I call everyone babe."

His eyelids lowered a fraction, and he pulled me closer. "No need to apologize. I don't think it's weird at all. I think it's endearing."

Double shoot.

Now men were interested in me? Now that I couldn't do anything about it while in the program? Thick dark hair, sleepy dark bedroom eyes, tall muscular body...life was so unfair. What had I done that was so bad to be punished like this?

I did not need this kind of trouble right now. "Listen, I—"

"May I cut in?" came a male voice from behind me.

I shivered. Now *there* was trouble with a capital B.

"Save me a dance for later." Jinwoo bowed, pressed a kiss to the back of my hand, and gave Byron a head nod as he walked away.

Byron took me into his arms. "You look lovely, Ms. Jones."

"Thank you for the compliment, but..." I narrowed my eyes, "...I was handling that just fine myself, Mr. Storm."

"I don't know what you're talking about. I *am* your plus one, remember? I simply wanted to dance with my date."

"Right." I ignored the fact of how good it felt being held in his arms. "And this had nothing to do with a certain judge you were talking to?"

"We actually didn't talk about you at all," Byron looked me in the eye to drive his point home, "but he *is* watching you."

"Then I guess I'd better be on my best behavior." I glanced over to find Zander indeed watching me with knowing eyes.

I winked at him.

He frowned and looked away.

Byron sighed. "And there you go again, deflecting."

"And this is why I've been avoiding you, Yoda."

He arched a brow. "Yoda?"

"You and your Jedi mind tricks."

"I'm more of a Luke."

"You are no Luke. If we're being totally serious, you're definitely Han, and I don't know how much more I can take." The music came to an end.

He spun me around and then dipped me. "Well, Princess, you're stuck with me. This program has only just begun."

Chapter Six

"So tell me, everyone, how is your journey going on making amends to those you have done wrong to?" Dr. Hastings sat in our group circle with her notebook in hand. She looked around the room, waiting for one of us to share. It was just the six of us again.

"Men are just awful." Misty blinked back tears from her amber eyes.

"Not everyone will be open to forgiving you that easily." Shirley gave her a sympathetic look. "Just keep trying. That's all we ask of you."

"Oh, the football team has no problem forgiving me and offering to do way more than that." Misty threw her hands up and shook her blonde ponytail. "How am I supposed to say no to that?"

"You're not alone. Bring your sponsor with you next time. Just remember why you're making amends and stay strong. You'll get there." Shirley turned to Bernard. "How are things going, Bernie?"

"Okay, I guess. I've made amends with several of the women in my retirement community, but the one who matters most still hasn't forgiven me." He scrubbed a hand through his thick head of silver hair, his gray eyes a little sad. "Karma, I guess."

"Give her time and yourself some grace. Change doesn't happen overnight." Shirley smiled kindly at him.

He nodded. "Problem is I'm not getting any younger."

"Neither is she. I have a feeling she'll come around." Shirley looked around the group. "How about you, Mae? Did you make any progress?"

"I did." She smiled shyly, her black and gray hair loose instead of in its usual bun. She adjusted her spectacles. "My husband is willing to compromise and try new things if I'm willing to slow down so I don't give him a heart attack." She covered her lips with her fingertips and stifled a giggle as she blinked rapidly. "It's not too bad abstaining. It's allowing us to grow closer by really talking and getting to know each other all over again. I didn't realize how much I missed that."

"That's wonderful, Mae. I'm so happy for you. Keep up the good work." Shirley looked at Lorenzo. "How's the job at the museum going?"

"Well, I'm not getting fired by my uncle because I've stopped watching porn." He shrugged. "I wouldn't say he's forgiven me, though."

"Not firing you is a good sign." Shirley nodded.

"I have some women on my list I need to apologize to, if they'll even see me. It's been a while since we've spoken."

"You would be surprised how much it means to hear someone say I'm sorry and mean it." She smiled. "Just keep moving forward."

"Well, I'm not sorry. The women at my bakery love me, capiche?" Duke Romano lifted his huge hands, palms up. "My mama is the only one who has a problem with me. I said I was sorry to her, but she knows I'm really not."

"Making amends comes in many forms. If you've upset your mother, then she deserves to hear you *honestly* repent your actions. And how do you know none of the women you've been with are upset with you?"

"What's upsetting about all this, Doc?" He gestured up and down his body with a half-cockeyed grin slanting across his face.

"Maybe that you're sharing all *that* with other women?" She kept her face non-judgmental and her voice calm.

He blinked and his eyes widened. "You mean like one of them might be upset about sharing me because they're in love with me?"

"You said it yourself. You are pretty special. It stands to reason that some of the women might think that by giving yourself to them that you think they are special, too," Dr. Shirley said carefully. "Sorry or not sorry, it is your job to own how you make others feel. Do you think you can do that?"

He nodded. "I have to admit I never thought of it that way. I can try to make amends, and I will try to do better communicating in the future."

Do. Or do not. There is no try, I thought as I channeled Yoda.

"That's all anyone can ask." Shirley looked at me as if she'd read my mind. "Would you care to share your progress, Ms. Jones?"

I wanted to say the only thing I was sorry about was that half the men in Mayflower were idiots, but I knew my sentence wasn't over until Dr. Shirley Hastings said I had successfully completed the 12-step program.

So, I donned a remorseful expression. "Help me, Dr. Obi—er, Shirley. You're my only hope."

She narrowed her eyes. "May the Force be with you, Princess."

Oh, she was good. "I'm just saying I might need a little luck."

"A wise man once said, 'In my experience, there's no such thing as luck.'" She quirked a brow. "Are we done now?"

"Sorry." I crossed my arms. "I'm not feeling much like a princess lately." I blew out a frustrated breath. "Old rivals and new rivals are still wreaking havoc on my life. And no matter what I say, the men in my town that I *wounded* don't believe anything I say. Look, I know I can be a little over-the-top. I can admit that and will gladly apologize, but no one lets me get close enough to say so."

"And why is that?" She stared at me with the same all-knowing gaze that Byron gave me. Must be a therapist thing.

"I own a new age shop with all sorts of unique, cool things inside. I find witchcraft fascinating. Yes, I dabble at practicing the craft, but I dabble at a lot of other things as well like psychic tools to predict the future. That doesn't mean I'm a real psychic or witch. I don't cast spells on anyone, but believe me, some of them deserve it. Someone is trying to ruin me, and I don't know why."

"That's simple, don't let them," she said without hesitation as if it were that simple.

Was it that simple?

I blinked. "Easier said than done."

"Not really. Ignore the rumors and focus on you. Don't waste energy on things you can't control. It's pointless. Focus on controlling your own actions, and everything else will fall into place. Villains only spread rumors to get a rise out of their victims. If you don't give them the satisfaction of seeing you upset, then the rumors become pointless, and the villain fails. End of rumors."

She had a point.

The harder I tried to find the villain, the crazier the rumors got. Maybe if I ignored the rumors and went about my life as if they didn't affect me at all, then people would start to believe they were just hearsay, and the rumors really would stop.

It was worth a shot.

"Thanks, Doc." It was kind of nice having an objective

person see things I couldn't. "Maybe there's some benefit to this group stuff after all."

She laughed out loud at that one. "You're welcome...I think."

"Wow, this French Onion Soup is amazing, doll." Tiffany pushed her spoon through the Gruyere cheese and toasted baguette on top of the caramelized onions and beef broth, scooping another bite into her mouth.

"Coq au Vin is to die for." Morticia cut a piece of chicken braised in red wine with mushrooms, onions, garlic and bacon that created a flavorful sauce. She added mashed potatoes before closing her lips around the fork and moaning as if her tastebuds were delighted.

I know mine were.

"The Ratatouille is delicious, babe." I sighed in heaven over the dish of tomatoes, zucchini, and bell peppers seasoned with herbes de Provence.

She'd also added Fromage plate—a selection of French cheeses like Brie, Roquefort, and Comte served with fresh baguette slices and some fruit like grapes and figs. I was more of a beer person, but even I appreciated the crisp Chardonnay wine she'd paired the meal with. It made the flavors pop.

"Thanks, ladies. Wait until you try the Crème Brulée for dessert. The creamy custard and caramelized sugar crust provides the perfect balance of smooth and crunchy textures." Zoe kept bringing more and more dishes to her kitchen table.

"Very smart choice in choosing Paris for your honeymoon." Tiff wiped the corners of her mouth daintily.

"Don't get me wrong, I'm grateful for this meal, but I hope you left room to play and didn't just work." Morti winked.

"Oh, trust me, hon. I took very good care of Chaz." Zoe's face transformed into a dreamy expression. "I love my children dearly and my job is so fulfilling, but it felt amazing to put ourselves first and do whatever we wanted for a change."

"That's awesome," I said and meant it. "We're all so happy for you. Chaz is a wonderful man." I nodded. "Trust me, they're hard to come by."

"What about Jinwoo?" Zoe's eyes sparkled with mischief. "You seemed to hit it off with him."

My jaw unhinged. "I knew something was up. Is that why you paired him with me at your wedding?"

Zoe was already shaking her head. "That was actually Chaz's idea. He knew you and Jin would be a good match. I personally am still rooting for Byron."

"Jin is definitely a handsome man, but Byron is more my type." The girls started to clap, but I held up my hand. "Not so fast, babes. I told you I am abstaining until my sentence is complete."

"And how's that working out for you, doll?" Tiff sipped her Chardonnay.

"Just fine."

"Of course, it's *just fine* because avoidance equals abstinence," Morti pointed out. "The moment you spend more than a minute alone with Studmuffin Storm will be the real test. 'Just fine' will take on a whole new meaning."

I frowned at her. "Do you want me to fail?"

She gave me a serious look. "I want you to be happy. Screw Zander. I'm sick to death of guys calling all the shots."

Why did I feel like Morti's comment had more to do with her than me?

Zoe squeezed my hand. "We all do."

I blinked. "Do what?"

Zoe studied me curiously. "Want you to be happy."

"Then let me do this my way. I need to prove I can make it through this program. I shouldn't care what this town thinks of me, but I do." And I refused to let Zander win. "Besides, if Byron were going to make a move, he would have done so by now, but he hasn't. It doesn't matter how I feel if he doesn't feel the same way."

"He hasn't made a move because he's a professional, like you said," Tiff pointed out. "That doesn't mean he doesn't want to."

I pointed my finger at her. "Or he's simply still here because he owes Zander a favor." Besides, I couldn't risk him rejecting me, too.

"That must be some debt he owes Zander." Morti's brow puckered.

"Exactly." I nodded.

I was dying to know what it was, but that would

involve talking to Byron. No matter what I said...that was dangerous territory for me. Because no matter how he felt about me, I knew exactly how I felt about him.

I shook my head. "He's only here because of a favor. I'm sure he'd be long gone if he could, so I'm doing him a favor by avoiding him." I looked them each in the eye, making it clear I was tired of this topic. "And that's all I'm going to say about that."

"Speaking of avoiding people," Morti interjected, taking the hint. "Dear ole Dad has been MIA lately. I've had to pick up the slack at the funeral home, leaving me very little time for myself. I've missed two meetings these past couple weeks."

"Meetings?" Tiff clapped her hands. "Did you finally join a group around town? That's so exciting, Morti."

"Yes and no." Morticia wouldn't meet our eyes.

"Let me guess." I studied her closely. "Yes, you joined a new group, and no, it's not around town."

"Oh, no, Morti." Zoe sighed. "Another online book club?"

"What's wrong with that?" Morti sat up straighter.

"Like you said, we want you to be happy." I sipped my Chardonnay, ready to switch to beer. "Online strangers and dead people do not equal happiness, Morti. Have you thought of joining an in-person club?"

"Why?" She shrugged. "I have you girls when I need an in-person connection. Like *I* said, I'm sick of men dictating what happens in our lives."

"Is everything okay, Morti?" I asked. She was definitely not herself lately.

"Of course. Why wouldn't it be?" She didn't make eye contact.

"Just checking. Zoe is busier than ever, Tiffany has her hands full with the twins, and I'm in the middle of a mess. I just worry about you being so alone, is all, especially with your father being MIA."

"I'll be okay. I'm sure he'll be back soon. I just wish he would have told me where he was going this time."

"Isn't it funny how the roles reverse the older we get?" I thought of my mother and her Bedazzled Boomers group and my father with his lumberjack games. "Our parents have more of a social life than we do, and we're the ones sitting home worried about what they're getting themselves into next."

"I try not to know what my parents and ex-in-laws are up to." Zoe shuddered. "It's downright scary."

"I've never had to worry about that, but I have to say, I'm loving getting to know mine." Tiffany smiled.

"Give it time," Zoe and I said simultaneously and laughed.

"I don't even have that." Morti sighed.

The rest of us made eye contact. Something was going on with her, but she was such a private person, even with us. She'd become more reclusive than ever, and we were more and more worried every day.

We just had no clue what to do about it.

Chapter Seven

"Hey, Harm. Glad you could come, honey. It means the world to your mother to have her entire family here for her seventieth birthday party." My father, Arnold, gave me a bear hug, nearly busting out the seams of his flannel shirt and straining his suspenders.

Paul Bunyan had nothing on my lumberjack dad. He was still a striking man with his thick salt and cayenne-pepper hair and beard. He had always been my rock. A big softie with open arms and a bear hug whenever I needed it. He didn't care that I was a tomboy. He never tried to change me, unlike my mother.

I just wish I was enough for her.

Shaking off that depressing thought, I gave him a genuine smile. "I wouldn't miss it, Dad. Can't believe Mom got all seven boys and their families to come today." I squirmed in the dress I'd worn to make her happy.

My mother, Wanda, was a bit obsessed with me. I

knew she loved me, but she was very demanding. The male gene was very dominant in our family. She had seven sons in seven years before finally giving up hope.

Until three years later, I came along.

Six of my brothers were now married and had fourteen sons among them between the ages of sixteen and two. The only one who wasn't married was my youngest brother, Homer, who had been holding out hope for Tiffany. Now that she was engaged to Matt, Homer had finally moved on and even had a girlfriend.

I was my mother's only hope for a granddaughter.

I wasn't even sure that I wanted children, but I didn't have the heart to tell her. So occasionally I gave her a gift by wearing a dress. I didn't own any, but Tiffany let me borrow a pale green one that matched my eyes. I was only five-foot seven to Tiff's five-foot ten and built like a boy compared to her measurements, but she had assured me this was a long sleeve, body hugging number that would adjust to my measurements perfectly. That was what she loved most about it.

It was pretty much one size fits all.

I had to admit her tip on the push-up bra was ingenious. I had always been comfortable in my own skin, but for the first time I could remember, I felt sexy. I'd even relented and allowed Morti to slick back my short hair and do my makeup. She'd given me a smokey eye and lined them to make them even more catlike. Clear lip gloss finished off the look. Zoe lent me big hoop earrings and bangle bracelets.

I had to admit that I didn't hate the look.

My mother came down the stairs of the massive farmhouse on the outskirts of town I had grown up in. The house sat on fifteen acres with woods covering most of that. We didn't actually have a farm, but my father, brothers, and I used the land during all four seasons. We hunted, hiked, drove four wheelers, and snowmobiles during my entire childhood. We had a pool out back and my father had built a roof and outdoor bar onto the patio over the years, and now the grandchildren were having the same fun we did and making memories.

Mom's eyes lit up when she saw me.

I smiled and curtsied.

Tears threatened to spill over the corners of her eyes as she whispered, "You look beautiful, sweetheart."

"Aww, thanks, Mom. It took a team, literally, but I'm kind of digging the results." I spun around and laughed. "Who knew?"

"I knew." She beamed a hopeful smile at me. "You should do it more often, dear. It suits you."

"Probably not." I swallowed a snort. Did she not know me at all?

Her smile slipped. "Well, that's a shame."

I relented a little. It *was* her day, after all. "At least I gave you today." I smiled, showing all my teeth.

"Well, that's at least something, isn't it." She patted my hand. "Thank you, dear. It means more than you know."

"You're looking stunning as always." I turned the subject off me.

She wore a sparkling copper gown that complemented her light brown hair. She'd swept the strands into a chic updo, and her green eyes sparkled with excitement as she touched the bedazzled crown she wore with matching earrings. "Aren't these just darling?"

"Very nice, Mother."

"I have a gift for you." She clapped her hands.

I narrowed my eyes. "But it's not my birthday. It's yours."

"Oh, believe me, it's a gift to me as well." She pointed behind me.

I turned around slowly and sucked in a sharp breath.

Byron Storm walked through the door and scanned the room, his eyes widening when he saw me, but then his mask settled back over his face as he made a beeline in my direction. He wore a burgundy suit with tapered legs that came to a stop just above his shiny black dress shoes with no-show socks. He'd left the top two buttons of his black dress shirt unbuttoned with no tie. His hair was pulled back into a man bun, and the scent of his earthy cologne hit me when he came to a stop by my side.

I took a moment to drink in the sight of him.

"Wow," was all I managed to get out.

His lips tipped up slightly at the corners. "Compliments of Dr. Chaz." His gaze ran over every inch of me and for once, I saw a sliver of what he was feeling. "You look beautiful, Harmony."

"Thanks. Compliments of all my girls." I smoothed a

hand down the front of my dress. "No way I could have pulled this off alone."

"I don't know." His eyes met mine and held me captive. "I'm pretty sure you can accomplish anything you set your mind to."

"What are you doing here?" I swallowed hard.

"Your mother said you needed a date."

"I would have called you if I did."

"Would you have?" He paused a beat. "Because you've been pretty radio silent lately. Did I do something to upset you?"

"No. I asked for your thoughts, and you gave them to me. I've just been busy." And terrified of what else he might see inside my head. The man was very good at his job. Or just very good at reading me.

"Fair enough, but I am here for you. If you need anything at all, just say the word. That's the whole point of me renting the cottage."

I wasn't ready to analyze everything that was going on inside my head. Need him? If only he knew what I really needed from him, he would go sprinting back to Boston as fast as he could.

"I'll try to remember that." I looked anywhere but at him.

"Good. All I want to do is help. Any more luck making amends?"

"One man accepted my apology. Another man apologized to *me*." I shook my head. "Said he was just messing with me because I'd turned him down in the past." I shrugged. "But Peter is still acting like I'm Darth Vader."

"We can't all be Obi-Wan. He'll come around eventually. Some people just take more time than others."

"I know I'm supposed to care that he does come around, but I don't." My gaze finally met his again. "I just need Dr. Shirley to believe I'm reformed."

"And that's why you need my help." He stared at me for a long moment. "No more ghosting me, okay?"

I blew out a long, slow breath. "Okay."

"Good." He looked around curiously. "Who are all these people anyway?"

"My brothers and their families."

He blinked, taking a moment to scan the room. "All of them? I thought maybe some were cousins."

"Nope. Only six women plus me and my mother. Then seven sons, fourteen grandsons, and my father."

"Wow, I will never complain about my two sisters, three nieces, and my mother again." His expression was pure fascination. "This actually explains a lot about you."

"Exactly." I threw my hands up. "Finally, someone who understands. How can I be any other way than how I am with these knuckleheads as role models?"

"Let's not forget the pressure you put on yourself," he reminded gently.

"I don't know what you're talking about. Enough about my brain." I grabbed his hand and ignored the zing of electricity I felt. "Come with me, and I'll introduce you to the Jones gang. Their brains will keep you busy for a lifetime."

Or at the very least for the remainder of his stay in Mayflower. Because one thing was certain...

I couldn't risk Byron Storm getting into my heart.

"Do you think he'll show?" I looked out the window at *Lolita's Place,* but still no sign of Peter.

I'd taken Byron up on his offer to play mediator in my third attempt to make amends with Peter, because clearly, I wasn't getting very far on my own. Byron had suggested someplace public to make Peter feel more comfortable. I mentioned *Lolita's Place* because everyone went there.

Al and Walt were there. I overheard them talking about their booths for the spring festival, but they didn't say one word about me. Probably because last time I saw them I hinted that I would put a curse on them. Byron had been right.

My mouth was my own worst enemy.

Rose was there with Phoenix, of all people, discussing a new display for the historical literature section Rose wanted in the library. Of course, Phoenix had just the antiques she was looking for. Neither of them would so much as glance in my direction.

Speaking of rivals. I focused back on Lolita.

We went to high school with her. She and Morticia had always been at odds since Morticia was chosen instead of her to be on the cheer squad. Over the years, whatever Morti had, Lolita wanted. Now that Lolita was dating

Officer Pickles, she and Morti had finally called a truce of sorts. No one could deny her restaurant was the best. Not to mention I could accomplish multiple goals.

Make PeeWee comfortable and show everyone I was trying to do the right thing.

I'd learned the hard way that things got twisted when they were done in private. I needed witnesses to my "amending" if Dr. Shirley was ever going to give me the *all clear* so I could resume my life. Byron had set up the lunch date, and Peter had agreed to come...

Yet he hadn't shown up.

"I don't see why Peter wouldn't show," Byron answered my question. "He has nothing to lose and every-thing to gain. A free meal and an apology."

"Exactly." I slapped the table with my palm, growing frustrated. "It's a no brainer...so where is he?"

"You're not a very patient person, are you?" He leaned to the side and glanced at my knee as it bounced up and down then raised a brow at me.

I sighed. "No, I'm not." I forced my leg to stop shaking. "I have a lot riding on this. I just want this program to be over with already."

He paused a moment as if choosing the proper words then looked me in the eye. "Real change takes time, Harmony."

I shook my head. "I promise you I'm not a sex addict."

"I'm not talking about that," he added gently.

I sat back and crossed my arms. "And I'm not ready to talk about the problems with my mother."

"Fair enough." He nodded.

"What about you?" I studied him like he always did me.

He frowned. "What do you mean?"

This time I made him wait. "What exactly did Zander do for you to make you drop everything and do him a favor this big to uproot your life for months?"

Byron's eyes flashed with something, but then they resumed their normal, unreadable expression. "It's no big deal. I had some free time, so I said yes. Besides, I find your case fascinating."

"Now who's deflecting?"

His lips tipped up slightly as if he were amused, but then the bells over the front door rang as someone walked in.

"Saved by the bell," I muttered.

He chuckled but didn't respond as he waved at Peter.

Peter made his way over to us. Just when things were getting interesting. Good ole PeeWee never did have the best timing. He sat on the side next to Byron, as far away from me as possible. This time at least he took his jacket off.

Progress.

"Glad you could make it, Peter." Byron handed him a menu.

"Thanks." Peter scanned the menu and then looked up at me as if daring me to say something smartass as he added, "I got held up helping my mother."

It took everything in me to resist the urge. He made it

so easy. "That's okay. We didn't mind waiting." I smiled. "Right, Mr. Storm?"

A muscle in Byron's cheek twitched, but he wisely didn't point out I had been anything but patient. "Not at all. Do you guys know what you want?"

The waiter came by, and we placed our orders. Byron and I ordered a beer, and Peter ordered an Old-Fashioned. Maybe I had misjudged him. Maybe he had a little Han Solo in him after all.

"Look, Peter, you don't have to forgive me, but I at least hope you will hear me out." I spoke with the sincerest tone I could muster.

He finally looked at me. Really looked at me. "I'm listening."

"I never meant to upset you. I promise you, I'm not a witch. Maybe I came on a little over the top, but that is only because I'm so frustrated with these rumors. They're not true, and totally unfair."

He stared at me for a long moment, and then nodded. "I get that." He took a sip of his Old Fashioned, studying me above the rims of his glasses. "Believe me, I know what it's like to be misunderstood."

I looked at him in a new light. "I believe you, and I'm sorry if I ever judged you unfairly. This whole dating scene is impossible in this town."

"You're telling me." He grunted. "My *mother* is impossible."

I gaped. "Yours too?"

"You have no idea."

"Trust me, I think I do."

"Cheers to that." He raised his glass.

"May our meddling mothers mind their own business." I clinked my glass to his.

"May the Force be with you both." Byron raised his own glass and took a sip.

We all laughed.

"I'd say you two turned a corner today." Byron looked between the two of us.

"I would have to agree." Peter studied me. "You're not so bad after all, Harmony Jones. Truce?"

"Truce." I nodded, adding, "Friends?"

He arched a brow. "Don't push your luck."

"Fair enough." At least the evening had gone far better than I had hoped, and that was a start.

Chapter Eight

"What a fine first day of March this is." Mayor Edwards walked through the front doors of *Peace, Love & Harmony*. He wore his standard white linen suit, curving over his rounded belly, and smiled wide at me with apple cheeks.

"It sure is." I smiled back, taking a deep cleansing breath of the aromatherapy candles I had burning. It was most definitely a good day so far, with hopefully no more drama. Things had finally started to quiet down a little. I turned down the new age music in the background. "What can I do for you, Mayor?"

"Well, it's Eleanor's and my fortieth wedding anniversary. I would really like to get something special for her. I've given her all the usual things like flowers, perfume, and jewelry. Your shop has such unique items, I was hoping you could help me pick out something different for her."

"Absolutely." I tapped my chin as I looked around,

studying my supplies. "Let's see. I just got a new collection of essential oils in. They smell wonderful and there's an oil for pretty much anything you're looking for. Health ailments. Sleep aids." I lowered my voice. "Mood enhancers."

His cheeks flushed candy apple red. He cleared his throat and scanned my shop as if making sure we were alone. "Well, thank you, Ms. Jones. If you could, er, point me in the direction of the last one, I would be most obliged."

"Good choice." I winked. "Follow me, sir. I will hook you up."

"Okay, um, but nothing too crazy, mind you."

"Of course not." I waved my hand. "Don't worry. I've got you." I was proud of myself for refraining from adding, *Babe.*

The struggle was real.

He followed me to the far wall, which housed all my essential oils.

"Thank you for your help, Ms. Jones. I really appreciate it. This is all so intimidating; I wouldn't know where to begin." He adjusted the lapels of his suit. "Just want to keep the spark alive with the Mrs. and all."

"You don't have to explain anything to me, Mayor." I patted his arm. "I'm happy to help all my customers, whatever their needs might be."

"What are all of these for, anyway?" He scratched his bald head.

I picked up a bottle. "Well, this here is called Ylang-

ylang. It has aphrodisiac properties and creates a calming and sensual atmosphere."

"That sounds all right." He nodded, looking a little wary but still open. "What about this one." He pointed to another bottle.

"That one is jasmine. Love and romance surround this little guy. It's sweet, exotic scent can uplift and arouse its user. Definitely a crowd pleaser."

"Oh, my." He fanned his chubby cheeks.

"And this one here is rose. Everyone knows a rose symbolizes love and passion, with its floral scent that creates a romantic ambiance."

"That might be more my speed," he admitted, then added, "although I've given her roses before. What else do you have?"

"Sandalwood." I picked up another bottle. "It has a warm, woody aroma that can promote relaxation and intimacy."

"Oh, lavender." He grabbed a small amber bottle and examined it with pleasure. "Eleanor loves lavender. What does it do?"

"It's primarily known for its calming effects, but it can also create a soothing and romantic environment."

"What is *this* one?" His eyes lit up as his gaze locked in on another bottle. He picked it up, looking intrigued.

"That is my favorite. It's Patchouli. I love its earthy scent. It's believed to have aphrodisiac qualities, making it a popular choice for romantic settings among my clientele."

"Sold. I'll take that." He lowered his voice. "And maybe a bottle of that ying yang one with a little jasmine on the side. May as well cover all my bases." His eyes twinkled like a dog in a butcher shop.

"Certainly. I'll add *Ylang-ylang* and jasmine to your order," I waggled my eyebrows, "and throw in a book on Kama Sutra."

His candle apple cheeks turned to the color of beets, but he didn't look away. "It will be our little secret, of course."

"Discretion is my middle name." I packaged up his order and did a double take when I noticed his expression change. He was staring at the shelf behind me with his lips parted and his eyes bugging. I glanced over my shoulder but didn't see anything amiss. "Is something wrong, Mayor?"

His eyes widened further, and he quickly shook his head. "N-No. Everything is just fine. I wouldn't want to do anything to upset you."

I handed him his package and arched a brow high. "You don't want to do anything to upset me? First of all, I doubt that you could, but more importantly, why would you be afraid to? What's going on, Mayor?"

He swallowed hard and pointed at the shelf behind me.

I turned around fully and looked at a wall of random items I hadn't found a place for yet. I crossed my arms and studied the wall then threw my hands up as I faced him once more. This was getting a bit ridiculous. "I'm not sure what you see that's so upsetting. Can you be more specific?"

He bit his bottom lip and then huffed around my counter to point to a lower shelf. "That right there."

I looked again. "I really don't know what you're..." My mouth gaped.

Shock ran through me. This was taking things way too far. There on the shelf wedged between various items was a Voodoo doll. Some traditional Voodoo dolls were crocheted, while others were made of corn stalks, and this one was made of clay. I'd never seen one in person. I read books about a lot of things I found interesting.

"I-Is that..." He couldn't seem to finish his sentence as if he were in a Harry Potter movie and we weren't allowed to say the name of the evil villain out loud.

It looked exactly like Judge Zander Jackson.

"It sure looks like *him*," was all I said, suddenly leery to say *his* name myself. How on earth did that get there?

"Are those pins stabbed all over his back?" The mayor's voice went up an octave and his face grew pale.

"It sure looks that way." I ground my teeth, growing angrier by the minute, feeling as though I'd been violated... or at least my space had.

"Looks painful if you ask me." His wary gaze met mine, his face growing paler by the second. "I, um, wouldn't want you to make one of those of me, so I'll just be taking my packages and be on my way."

I shook my head. "But that's not even mine." I grabbed the doll and held it up before his face.

"It's in *your* shop. Who else would it belong to?" He backed quickly toward the door, shaking his head. "I don't want any trouble."

"Neither do I," I blurted, adding, "Discretion, remember?" to his retreating back, hoping he heard.

The last thing I needed was for people to think I went around making Voodoo dolls of people who pissed me off. Now people were going to think I was a high priestess, for crying out loud. I did *not* go around stabbing pins in dolls to hurt people, using black magic to get revenge on them.

It didn't matter.

People had seen too many movies to believe otherwise. I looked out the window and blinked. Oh, my goddess, this was not good. So much for no more drama. Heather Hunnicut was staring through my window, her mouth hanging open, with her eyes trained on the Voodoo doll of Zander I clutched in my hand.

"A Voodoo doll?" My mother set a large French toast casserole on the table beside a ham and Swiss quiche for our weekly Sunday brunch after mass. "For Heaven's sake, what were you thinking, Harmony?"

I was thinking I should have stayed home and skipped church today. I had my own way of worshipping, but I kept trying in vain to make my mother happy. I sighed. "For the millionth time, it's not mine."

"Honey, that nasty thing was in your shop." She shuddered as she added a bowl of fruit to the table. "Of course it's yours."

"Of course. Silly me for not knowing what's mine." I threw my hands up and shook my head as my sarcasm sailed right over my mother's.

She tsked. "Poor Mayor Edwards had to go to the doctor for heart palpitations yesterday. That's why he wasn't in church today."

"I highly doubt his palpitations were from the doll," I mumbled, distinctly remembering a certain book I had blessed him with.

"What do you mean?" my father asked, glancing up at me as he passed around a bowl of hot crossed buns.

"I'm not at liberty to say. Unlike the mayor, *I* have discretion." I zipped my lips and threw away an imaginary key then leaned back and crossed my arms.

"Dude, you're not a doctor." Homer snorted and helped himself to more eggs. He didn't even go to church. He just showed up for the food. The rest of my siblings hadn't arrived yet. Late as usual yet never in trouble.

"When my customers ask for confidentiality, I oblige them," I spoke to him slowly and carefully as if he were a child. He was certainly acting like one. "It's good business and keeps them coming back for more."

My father grunted. "That must have been some purchase he made. Maybe you should hook your old man up with whatever you gave him."

"You'll do no such thing, Arnold." My mother frowned at him, swatting him on his muscular arm. "I don't need you ending up in the hospital with *any* part of you palpitating like poor Mr. Edwards."

My father just winked at her.

I blew out a breath. "The mayor didn't end up in the hospital because of anything I did. If you want to point fingers, blame the real culprit who put the doll in my shop. To create a doll that looks exactly like Zander with pins stabbing him in the back is totally meant to set me up. This is not going to go over well in a town like Mayflower."

"I'm sure it will blow over, Bean. Just keep your head down." My father lightly punched me in the shoulder. He'd always called me Bean, short for string bean, on account of my being tall and skinny like a beanpole. I had thought I would outgrow the teenage boy look, but that never happened.

My mother shook her head at him and then looked at me. "A lady doesn't cause trouble. Maybe refrain from some of your unusual hobbies for a while. Act more normal, and people will find something else to talk about."

"I like my uniqueness," I shrugged, "but I promise you I don't make Voodoo dolls, Mother." I inhaled a deep breath and counted to ten before I said something I might regret. I wish she could see her version of normal didn't make it the only acceptable version. "The doll creator has to be the same person spreading rumors that I'm a witch."

"Well...aren't you?" Homer arched a brow at me and then smirked. "Oh, wait. That starts with the wrong letter. My bad."

I threw a banana at his head. "Bro, you are *not* helping."

"Harmony, honestly. We don't throw food at the table. That's what I'm talking about. Not very ladylike, indeed." She dabbed the corners of her mouth with her linen napkin. "You should know better."

"Sorry." My shoulders slumped. She had an uncanny way of making me feel fourteen instead of forty.

"Oh, dear, don't slouch. It's not good for your spine. You have to think about these things at your age."

This time my father frowned at my mother and shot me a look of sympathy. I didn't know which was worse. My mother's comments or my father's pity or my brother's idiocy. One thing I did know...I'd had enough for one day.

I snapped my spine straight, feeling ancient. I glanced at my watch. "Oh, look at the time. I have a meeting."

"On a Sunday?" My mother blinked. "But everyone isn't here yet. Surely whoever you're meeting with isn't as important as your family."

"We all live in the same town, Mom. I see my family all the time." Whether I wanted to or not.

"Well, if we're too boring for you, then don't let us stand in your way." She brushed imaginary lint off her Sunday best.

"The meeting is with my sponsor."

"Byron's cool." Homer nodded.

"And handsome." My mother sighed dreamily, her disappointment over me leaving early immediately forgiven.

"He's her sponsor." My father glared at the other two.

"Exactly, and he's waiting for me as we speak." I stood. "I would wait for the boys, Mother, but I don't want to keep Mr. Storm waiting too long."

"Go, go. Don't you worry about us. Enjoy your date with *Byron*." She beamed her giddiness palpable.

"It's a therapy session," I muttered as I headed to the door.

"Put on some mascara, dear. It will make your eyes pop, so you'll look less tired," was the last thing I heard as I closed the door firmly behind me.

I took the first easy breath since I got there, and then quickly climbed into my car and just started to drive. I knew my family meant well, but they were a lot on a good day. And today hadn't been a good day.

Not wanting to run into anyone else who might have heard about the doll, I kept driving and found myself at the end of Lighthouse Lane in front of Quincy Cottage on Freedom Lake. Byron was my sponsor, after all, and maybe Zander was right. I was in dire need of some extra therapy at the moment.

I pulled my jacket closed as I walked up Byron's sidewalk. March in the Northeast had a tendency to come in like a lion and out like a lamb. This late snowstorm was proof of that. Taking a chance he might be home, I knocked.

I heard movement inside and then the door opened.

Byron stood there in a pair of low-riding sweatpants and a short-sleeve t-shirt, revealing his intricate tattoo sleeve. His honey-brown hair was loose from his standard low ponytail, brushing his shoulders in thick waves. He ran a hand through the top as he opened the door wide and raised a brow at me.

I entered, rubbing the chill from my arms, no words necessary.

He closed the door behind me. "Make yourself at home. I just lit a fire."

I kicked off my boots and peeled off my coat before making a beeline for his couch. "Thanks. It's freezing out there."

"And tomorrow everything will melt. Gotta love spring in Massachusetts." He walked into his kitchen. "Can I get you something to drink? Water? Coffee or tea?"

"Got anything stronger?"

He refrained from looking at the clock. It was barely noon, but hey, it was five o'clock somewhere. Nodding once, he turned to a cabinet above the sink and pulled down a bottle of whiskey and two rocks glasses. Pouring us each a couple fingers, he carried them over and handed one to me before taking the seat beside me on the couch.

"Rough morning?"

"Rough week."

"Care to tell me about it?"

"That could take all day."

"I'll grab the bottle."

Chapter Nine

"So...tell me what's going on." Byron leaned back against the couch cushions with his bare feet crossed at the ankles and propped on the coffee table in front of us beside the half-empty whiskey bottle.

Oh, my goddess, even the man's feet were gorgeous!

I leaned back against the cushions as well, propping my own sock clad feet next to his while cradling my whiskey glass. "I don't even know where to start."

"I'm guessing this has to do with a Voodoo doll of Zander?" Byron looked at me questioningly, but with no judgment.

I groaned. "Please tell me he doesn't know about the doll?" How embarrassing. That would make Judge Jackass drum up even more bogus charges to bring against me. He must be loving every minute of his revenge.

Byron winced. "I wish I could, but he's the one who told me." He took a sip of his whiskey.

"This is why I hate small-town living." I downed the rest of mine and held out my glass for more.

He grabbed the bottle from the coffee table and poured another couple of fingers into my glass, then set the bottle down, his arm brushing mine when he leaned back. "Why don't you tell me what happened? It might make you feel better."

I found it hard to think straight with the warmth of his muscular arm pressing against mine. I cleared my throat and moved an inch away until our arms were no longer touching. "I don't need one more person thinking I'm lying, thank you very much."

"It's not my job to—"

"Seriously, dude, can you for once give me your honest opinion?" Well, shoot, that came out harsher than I meant it to, but I couldn't help it. I shouldn't care what he thought about me, but I did. He was only here because he had to be.

Silence hovered between us.

"For what it's worth, yes, I do believe you. I don't think you created the Voodoo doll, and I don't think you're a witch. Unique, yes, but that's not a bad thing. That's interesting." His gaze held mine for a moment too long before he looked away and continued. "I do think someone might be trying to set you up. Who and why, I don't know, but I'm happy to help you try and figure that out."

"Great. So you agree, I don't need therapy."

"I didn't say that."

I tilted my head to the side as I looked at him again with narrowed eyes. "Then you *do* think I'm a sex addict."

"I didn't say that, either." He was so calm, cool, and collected. It drove me crazy. Just once I wanted to see him lose control.

"Then what are you saying, dude?" I jumped up and started pacing, feeling fidgety, needing some space from this all-seeing wizard. "You're so confusing. And frustrating, you know."

"Your relationship with your mother is affecting you more than you would like to admit even to yourself."

I stopped walking and gaped at him. It was as if my skin were translucent, and he could see what was on my insides. "My mother means well. She's fine. We're fine."

"You're not fine, and neither is your relationship with her." He patted the couch beside him. "Why don't you sit back down."

I eyed the couch warily. "Only if you top off my drink."

He did as I asked and handed me the drink without a word.

"Don't judge," I said as I sat back down beside him.

"I wouldn't dream of it."

I sighed, hating being vulnerable. I was so used to thinking I couldn't show weakness. That I needed to be tough so I could take care of myself and wouldn't get made fun of. "I don't like to talk about my relationship with my mother."

"That won't fix anything." His voice was sympathetic

and filled with understanding as he spoke with a quiet, soothing, inviting tone.

"Fine. I'll talk to you." I shrugged and then snorted. "I mean you need to start earning your pay, babe."

"And there you go with your sarcastic humor to deflect." He swirled the liquid in his glass before setting it down without taking a sip.

"Insults? That's your tactic?" I set my own glass down, the whiskey churning inside my unsettled stomach.

"Honesty," he said gently and nudged my leg with his, his gaze softening. "You asked for my honest opinion, and I gave it to you. You don't have to like it, but you might want to at least listen to it."

"Okay, okay, Yoda." I raised my hands, palms up, in front of me. "How am I supposed to fix this?"

"Talk to your mother."

"No way." I dropped my hands, already shaking my head. "She's sensitive. I hate to see her cry."

"You hate to disappoint her as well, so you put on airs instead of being your authentic self."

"Well, what do you expect." I started ripping the napkin under my glass into tiny little pieces. "It took her eight children to finally get a girl, but I'm not the type of girl she was hoping for. It's not all her fault. My father and brothers raised me to be a tomboy."

Byron's warm hand slid over mine until my fingers stilled. "Has she ever said you're not enough of a girl for her?"

"Of course not. I know she loves me, and she's a good

mother for the most part. I just can't be me around her without feeling like I'm letting her down."

"And that is why you need to talk to her. You can't fix anything if she doesn't know what she's doing is hurting you. Tell her how you feel. She might surprise you."

I blew out a big breath. "I'll think about it."

He squeezed my hand before letting go. "That's all I ask."

"What about you?" I looked him over, pondering Byron the man. "I'm guessing you weren't always a Jedi Master."

He laughed and angled his body toward me slightly. "What do you want to know? I'm an open book."

"Why do you owe Zander a favor?"

A brief flash of emotion crossed his face, but he masked it so quickly, I couldn't tell what exactly the emotion was. "Except for that chapter." He straightened his body away from me in a closed-off position. "Let's just say the page has been turned and the rest of my life has been a rewrite."

"Pleading the Fifth, I see."

"Something like that." He winked.

I raised a brow high. "Sounds like you could use some therapy, too."

"Touché." He raised his glass and clinked it to mine with a small smile playing at the corners of his lips.

"You sure you want to take me on...as a client, I mean." I bit my bottom lip. *Were we still talking about therapy?*

His gaze dropped to my lips for a brief second before looking back at me. "I think I can handle it."

"Okay, but if you cry *Uncle*, I'm going to say I told you so." Our bodies were touching on the couch, and an undeniable electricity passed between us. For the first time I saw what the girls had seen.

Interest...a spark...*desire*.

We just sat there, staring at each other for a moment, then his head started to lower slowly toward mine. Closer, closer. I could feel his breath on my face, smell his earthy cologne, see the flecks of gold in his eyes. My eyelids fluttered closed in anticipation...

The only thing that kissed my lips was a draft of cold air.

My eyelids fluttered open, and I saw a pained expression in his eyes for a moment before he cleared his throat and looked away. I swallowed hard and concentrated on regulating my breathing. What just happened?

I blinked slowly as the realization that Byron Storm had almost kissed me sank in.

"You are one of a kind, Harmony Jones," he finally got out.

"You have no idea, Byron Storm."

"Everything looks pretty good." Dr. Joy checked her notes. "Except that your blood pressure is creeping up, and your stress levels are a bit high. Is something or someone making you anxious more than normal?"

She looked at me with no-nonsense yet non-judgmental dark eyes, her dark hair cut short and chic. She shared the family practice with Zoe's husband, Chaz. While Chaz was casual with his dockers and sweater most days, Dr. Joy was all about tradition. She wore a starched and pressed white lab coat with her stethoscope ever present, hanging out of her pocket or around her neck.

I adored Chaz, but Dr. Joy was a badass boss lady, and I loved it.

"I'm sure you've heard the rumors."

She nodded. "But those aren't new."

"No, but the person starting the rumors came to play." I scowled.

"Ahh, the Voodoo doll."

"It's not mine. I didn't make it."

"Whoever said you did?" She arched a brow.

I blinked. "You believe me?"

"Of course I do. Why on earth would you be the one fanning the flames? That doesn't make any sense."

"Thank you!" I nearly bolted off the table to give her a hug.

"Whoever is doing these things isn't too bright."

"Maybe it's an ex of someone I dated. I did try to seduce a few questionable men in town, but I was desperate for *companionship* and the pickings were slim."

"And how are the pickings now?" Her lips twitched in a rare hint of a smile.

I blinked. "Um...you do know I'm going to Sexaholics Anonymous, right?"

"Oh, I know, but I've seen your therapist."

My jaw fell open, and I was at a loss for words. *Good grief, Charlie Brown.* Was everyone able to read my mind these days?

"The answer is probably not, but I'm your doctor. I know you quite well, and your face is quite expressive. I'm thinking your sponsor might be spiking your blood pressure." She wrote something in her charts.

I bit my bottom lip before admitting, "I'm not gonna lie, that is a distinct possibility, Doc. Problem is, I don't know what to do about it."

"That does pose a conundrum. Maybe go to the gym or take up hiking or try mountain biking or even tennis. Anything to release the tension. Monitor your blood pressure at home, and I want to see you back in a month. Can you do that for me?"

"I can try."

"Do better than try, Harmony. You have to take your health seriously now that you're getting older. This is your heart we're talking about."

"Okay, okay. I promise."

"Good." She nodded her head once. "I'll hold you to that. See you in a month." She picked up her chart and walked out the door of the exam room.

Mic drop.

Apparently, we were done.

I shook my head and chuckled on the inside as I slid off the table and headed for the door. Once I entered the hall, I headed for the exit, passing various exam rooms along the way. One door opened and I heard Chaz's voice as he held the doorknob, hovering in the doorway, saying something to a patient inside.

"Yes, I'm sure the cream I gave you will help the rash." Chaz was so patient with his patients.

The patient said something I couldn't make out.

"Some rashes look like little pinpricks. It's not that uncommon."

The patient said something else.

"I promise the muscle relaxers will help with the back pain. If there's not anything else, I really have to—"

The patient spoke again, louder this time, sounding familiar.

"I really don't think this has anything to do with a doll."

Wait one minute...

I stormed forward and poked my head under Chaz's arm so I could see into the room, startling him. "Zander Jackson, I should have known."

"Hey, she can't be in here," Zander sputtered.

"Back pain and a pinprick rash?" I narrowed my eyes at him. "You are *not* blaming this one on me."

Chaz took my arm and guided me back into the hall, shutting the door behind him. "Mr. Jackson is right. You can't be in there, Harmony. HIPAA laws exist for people's privacy. You know that."

"Fine, I'll go. But mark my words, his bad back and rash have nothing to do with the stupid Voodoo doll."

"I'm not at liberty to discuss a patient's medical condition, Harm. You know that as well." He frowned. "Why are you here anyway?"

"A physical with Dr. Joy," I muttered. "My blood pressure and stress are elevated." I glared toward the closed exam room door. "Gee, I wonder why?"

Chaz walked with me toward the front of the building. "Why don't you have Tiff squeeze you in for a massage?"

"That's not a bad idea."

"Maybe get some dinner at Lolita's after with Morti."

I shrugged one shoulder. "I could eat, I guess."

He glanced at his watch. "Zoe will be free later. You all could go to McGinny's after for a drink."

"That could work."

"I really do have to go, but Harm?"

"Yeah?"

"Keep your chin up. Things will get better in time. I mean, this charade can't go on forever. Eventually the real culprit is going to slip up and get caught."

"You're right. Thanks, Chaz." I waved goodbye and headed outside when it dawned on me. What if Zander was faking his bad back, and what if he had something like acupuncture to make it look like a pinprick rash?

What if Zander Jackson was the person who had started the rumors in the first place?

Chapter Ten

"Wow, you outdid yourself, Morti. I love Indian food." Tiffany filled her plate with a roti—whole wheat flatbread, steamed basmati rice, chana masala—chickpeas in a spicy tomato sauce, aloo gobi—potato cauliflower vegetable dish, cucumber raita yogurt, mango pickle chutney, then added a bowl of lentil dal soup.

"Thanks, Tiff." Morticia filled our glasses with a signature drink she chose. "This is Palm Wine toddy made from the sap of coconut and date palm trees. There's papad—thin crispy wafers and kheer—rice pudding for dessert."

"That sounds wonderful." Zoe took the glass from Morti.

I eyed the glass warily as I took mine from her as well.

Tiffany was all about the food.

"Don't worry, Harm, I have beer."

I laughed. "You know me so well, but hey, I always try everything at least once." I picked up my glass of wine.

"You're braver than me." She held up her diet cola. "To best friends and weekly girls' nights."

We all raised our glasses and said, "Cheers."

Morti's place hadn't changed in years. Blacks, whites, and grays with books everywhere and not much else. She liked simplicity, order, and continuity. Sometimes I just wanted to mess everything up...mess *her* up...so she would snap off her hamster wheel routine and live a little. I worried about her. We all did.

"I for one am very grateful for you babes." I set down the nearly full wine and popped a beer. "My life is a mess these days. If it weren't for you girls, I think I would be in an insane asylum right now."

"I heard about the Voodoo doll." Tiffany winced and finished the rest of her wine. "That's so creepy."

"You know they're not real. It's all Hollywood's fault." It made me so mad that people didn't do their homework. I mean if they wanted to frame me for doing something, then they at least could get their facts straight.

"Still, I love the concept. I'd like to make a doll of my ex and put the needles where the sun doesn't shine just to put a smile on my face." She winked. "It's the little things." A giggle slipped out.

"Amen to that, sister." Morti handed her a martini.

"Thanks, doll." Tiffany took the drink.

"Oh, now there's a thought." Zoe's amber eyes sparkled. "I have an ex that I wouldn't mind sticking a needle or two...hundred into." She laughed.

"As much as I don't like Zander, I didn't make a doll in

his likeness or stick anything into him. People in this town will believe anything."

"Chaz told me about your run-in with Zander at the doctor's office, but he wouldn't tell me any details. He's such a stickler when it comes to doctor-patient confidentiality." Zoe sipped the Chardonnay Morti gave her. "I love the man to pieces, but why does he always have to do the right thing?"

"Well, I'm no doctor, so I'm not bound by that oath. I'll tell you exactly what Zander did. He came in with a backache and a rash that had pinpricks all over it."

"Pinpricks?" Morti scrunched up her face.

"Yes...exactly like someone had stabbed hundreds of tiny needles into his back. I think he secretly had acupuncture and had a reaction. The perfect excuse to go to the doctors and spread even more rumors that the doll worked."

Tiff's eyes widened. "Do you think it might have worked?"

"Hell, no." I looked them each in the eye. "I think Zander is the one who started the rumors in the first place."

"Why would he do that?" Zoe looked skeptical.

"He's been looking for a way to get even with me for years."

"What are you going to do?" Morti's dark eyes filled with worry.

"Find a way to prove it. It's no longer about my sanity, it's about my health. The man makes my blood boil."

"Are you sure he's the problem, doll?" Tiffany's eyes twinkled with mischief. "Cuz I can think of another man who makes your blood boil in an entirely different way."

"Okay, so Zander makes my stress levels rise, but Byron most definitely makes my blood pressure spike." Visions of us sitting side by side, our bodies touching, flashed through my mind's eye. "We almost kissed."

"Yes!" Zoe clapped her hands. "That makes me so happy, hon."

"Not me. I'm more confused than ever."

"Why?" Tiff looked pensive. "I don't understand what the big deal is. No one has to know what goes on between the two of you."

"I will know. He's my therapist, not to mention, he still won't tell me why he owes Zander a favor. I feel like he was forced into this situation. I'll never know if he would leave if he could. I don't know. Maybe I was reading him wrong. Maybe he wasn't about to kiss me. Maybe I just imagined the look of desire in his eyes."

"I doubt it. Desire is pretty hard to mistake, even online." Morti blinked, then looked away as she blushed. "So, how are the babies, Tiff?"

"Doing great." Tiffany eyed her shrewdly.

"And the kids?" Morticia turned to Zoe.

"Getting ready for spring sports." Zoe studied her with a raised brow.

"You're not getting off that topic so easily." I stared Morti down. "Out with it, babe. What's going on with you these days?"

"My father had a suspicious spot on his prostate so that's why he was at the doctor's. I didn't want to say anything before he got the results, but he has cancer. That's why he's been sneaking away so much. He's been having treatments and didn't even tell me."

We all gasped.

"Oh, man, that sucks. At least it's prostate. Isn't that like a good cancer to get if you're going to get cancer? Not that any are good, but you know what I mean." I shrugged, trying to mentally pull my foot out of my mouth. I was so bad in these situations. My family drove me crazy, but I would be devastated if any of them ever got sick.

"I'm sure he didn't want to worry you, hon." Zoe squeezed her arm. "And Harm is right. Prostate cancer is one of the easier cancers to cure."

"I know. I'm trying to stay positive. I'm upset because he told Samantha and not me. I had to find out on my own through a pamphlet on his desk." Hurt flashed in Morti's eyes. "He would rather have her take care of him instead of me."

"Your father adores you. I'm sure he was just thinking of who would run the funeral home," Tiff pointed out logically.

"Yeah, Samantha can't do everything you do, Morti." I squeezed her hand. "Your father knows that. I'm sure he would have told you eventually."

"Maybe." She shrugged. "It's not just that. I really like this new online book club I'm in. I was finally flirting with a genuinely interesting man when all of this went down.

Now I don't have the time to devote to him, and he lost interest. Story of my life." Morti looked so sad and frustrated, my heart went out to her.

"It's spring. Anything is possible. Maybe the spring festival will bring new possibilities and a fresh start for you both." Zoe looked at Morti and me with a hopeful smile.

"Now there's the spirit." Tiff beamed along with her.

Morti snorted.

I rolled my eyes.

And the words *maybe not* whispered through my brain.

A WEEK LATER, it was officially spring, and the spring festival was on. Bitsy Beaumont was there with her principal husband and daughter. They had worked out their differences regarding the rules for their marriage and seemed happy. She oversaw the allocation of the town's funds for the festival, and even worked alongside Zoe amicably as she planned the party.

"We finally have some warm weather." Byron walked along beside me with his hands in his pockets as we entered the park.

I hadn't seen him since our *almost* kiss at the cottage during our therapy session. Everyone in town would be at the festival. They would expect to see me with my sponsor, so I wouldn't be tempted to attack any men—I mentally rolled my eyes—so I asked him to join me. At least that's the reason I told myself.

Not that I missed him or anything.

"I love it. Don't get me wrong, I love to ski and snowmobile, but I'm ready for some beach weather."

"Ah, you're a sun worshipper."

"More like a water fanatic."

"A woman after my own heart." He nodded, his mouth twisting into a lopsided grin. "I love the water, but I played tennis in college."

"Cool." I grinned back, shoving my own hands into my jeans pockets. "I was on the swim team, and I love to waterski."

"Sweet."

We fell into silence as we continued to walk.

It was a little too early for flowers to bloom fully, so our local flower shops provided the decorations of daffodils, tulips, daylilies, and peonies so the crowd could see what they had to look forward to very soon.

Zoe had great taste, so of course, everything looked spectacular.

Food trucks and craft tents were set up. Games were scattered about, and live entertainment was held on the stage by the gazebo. Matt McGinnis's cousin, Finn, was representing McGinny's Pub by playing his guitar and singing center stage while their other cousin, Aidan, manned the food truck along with their Uncle Liam.

Tiffany and Matt, along with their adorable twins, Declan and Genie, sat at a table with her parents, Rita and

Charlie Scott, and her twin sister, Tabatha. They had all made amends since the death of her Grammy and had become a big part of their lives now that the twins were born.

Tiff waved at me as we walked their way, and Matt gave Byron a head nod.

At the table next to them, Zoe sat with Chaz and their children, Lexi, Troy, Bobby, and Katy. Her parents retired in Florida and her ex-in-laws retired in Alabama. They weren't in town for this festival, but they would be here for Easter. Chaz's parents were also retired, but they still lived locally and sat with them.

Zoe shot me a big smile and clapped her hands when she saw Byron.

The next table over was Morticia, her father, and his girlfriend, Samantha. He sat between the two women, looking pale, and none of them looked very happy. Morticia looked up at Byron and me and relief swept over her features.

She flagged us down, waving us over wildly.

"Guess we know where we'll be sitting," I muttered.

"Guess so." He chuckled.

"Hey, guys, what's up?" I sat at the table across from the three of them, and Byron took the seat next to me.

"We're great. Everyone's great. Isn't this all just so great?" Samantha's face looked painful holding her smile that wide for so long.

Morticia rolled her eyes and shrugged. "I've been better."

Her father shot her a pleading look and then glanced at me with an expression just this side of painful, though I doubted his pain had anything to do with anything physical. He cleared his throat. "I'm glad the weather took a turn for the better."

"I know. I can't believe it snowed just a week ago." I shrugged, feeling the need to engage in small talk and cut the tension.

"You know what they say about March in our neck of the woods...in like a lion, out like a lamb." He lifted his hands.

"So I've seen. Your lake effect weather is something else." Byron shook his head. "I don't think we've officially met, sir."

"Sorry. I keep forgetting you're new to town." I looked at Byron sheepishly. "If feels like you've been here forever."

"Thanks, I think." He laughed and looked at Morticia's father as he held out his hand. "I'm Byron Storm."

"Harmony's therapist. I heard." Morticia's father winked at me. "I'm Mortimer Smith. Nice to officially meet you." He shook Byron's hand.

"Bet you thought his name was Gomez." Laughter peeled out of Samantha's mouth. Her hair was platinum blonde. Her body was tall and voluptuous. And she looked to be in her mid-forties.

Morticia rolled her eyes once more, harder if that were possible.

Morti looked like her father, except his eyes had turned

a softer dark brown and his hair was now more gray than black. She hadn't met her mother, but she'd seen pictures. She had been a petite, dark haired and dark eyed woman as well. Samantha was everything none of them were, and Morti was not a fan, judging by her body language and facial expressions.

The heart wanted what the heart wanted.

Change was hard, and Morti had never been a fan of change. Based on the conversations Morti had with me and the girls, I had a feeling she just didn't want to lose her father, too. Not to cancer, but to another woman. A woman the complete opposite of him. A woman far too young for him...

A woman who might be trying to take advantage of him.

"Hey, aren't those your friends?" Byron squinted close to me, looking off at a group of people headed our way, and my gaze followed his.

Oh. My. Goddess!

Misty Davenport, with her bottle-blonde ponytail bouncing along with her silicone implants, walked beside the petite Mae Chen, who sported a tennis visor and matching skort. Bernard Featherwood stood tall and distinguished as he walked with a cane he didn't need beside Lorenzo Gonzalez, who appeared bug-eyed as if he were reaching stimulus overload. The bald headed, jacked Duke Romano walked solo, in a league of his own, wearing tight black gym shorts and a tank top that looked like another layer of skin. By the way he strutted, he must have just pumped some serious iron.

Spotting me, they all waved excitedly, heading our way.

"Who's that?" Morti wrinkled her forehead as if trying to see them better. "I've never seen them in town before."

"Well, it *is* the spring festival, dear." Her father studied them. "A lot of outsiders come to Mayflower for many of our festivals."

"Yeah, but none who know my best friends."

I sighed. "They're from my SAA group."

"What kind of group is that?" Samantha asked, folding her hands on the table in front of her. "I've been looking for a new hobby."

"That's not the kind of group you're looking for, honey." Mortimer whispered something into her ear, and her face flushed a deep rose red."

"Isn't the A supposed to mean anonymous?" Morti raised a brow at me. "What are they doing here?"

"I have no clue. Apparently, in Mayflower, or any of the other small towns bordering her, *nothing* is anonymous." I pasted on a smile as they came to a stop beside our table, drawing several eyes from the locals surrounding us.

"Harmony, hi." Misty clapped excitedly.

"We're so glad you're here." Mae Chen folded her arms in front of her. "I wasn't sure you got the memo."

"You haven't been to a meeting in a while, so we didn't think you would know where to meet." Bernard rubbed his hands together, looking around with interest. "I have to say this festival was a wise choice. It looks positively full of temptation."

"Meet for what? I think I'm missing something." I didn't think I was going to like the answer.

"Our field trip. Go someplace none of us live and see how we do without prying eyes." Lorenzo shrugged. "It was Duke's idea."

"Yo, how else are we supposed to know if we can resist temptation without our sponsors around?" Duke folded his muscular arms until he saw Byron beside me, and then his eyes sprang wide. "Wait a minute. Isn't he your sponsor?"

"He sure is." I tried not to fidget as more eyes around the park turned my way. We were causing a scene, and I hated being the center of attention.

Byron tilted his head and gave a nod to the group.

Duke leaned in close to me. "Yo, toots, why is *he* here?"

"I didn't know about any field trip," I replied to the group, ignoring Dumbbell. "This is my town. I *live* here."

"Oh, well, why didn't you say so." Duke looked around at everyone staring at us. "Ohhhhh." He winced. "Sorry, toots. You weren't at the meeting to let us know. We'll pick another town."

Zander chose that moment to walk by, tsking and smirking every step of the way, casting all too knowing eyes in my direction.

"Don't bother. The damage is already done."

Chapter Eleven

"I can't believe the *Five Shades of Freakiness* showed up at the festival. I'm sure everyone in town knows I'm in SAA as my punishment for 'attacking Peter,' but still... we looked like freakshows on display for everyone to gawk over. I personally like my freakiness, but I didn't need the judgmental looks or comments this dinosaur of a town loves to give." I sipped my beer at McGinny's pub a week later.

The chatter *still* hadn't died down.

"I'm sure it wasn't as bad as you think, hon." Zoe patted my hand and sipped her Chardonnay.

"Did you see Zander's face?" I scowled at her. "He was loving every minute of it." I narrowed my eyes. "So much for the program being anonymous. I bet he made an *anonymous* call to Dr. Shirley, suggesting the *neutral* field trip." I looked over at Zander and Byron in deep conversation. The normal easy-going Byron didn't seem so laid back at the moment. He seemed frustrated, judging by the look on his face.

Good.

"Speaking of freakshows, Samantha has been trying way too hard to get me to like her." Morti sighed. "I don't dislike her, and I want my father to be happy. I'm just jealous, I guess." Morti wanted her father to need her like he used to. I could relate to longing for a parent's attention. "These days he barely remembers I'm around. He only has eyes for her. I just worry *her* eyes are trained on his bank account more than him. I just don't want to see him get hurt."

"What if she's genuine, and they actually do love each other?" I asked as gently as I could and tried not to wince. We could all see how smitten they both were. Morti just didn't want to believe her new mommy dearest could be someone her age.

"It probably is true, and I'm going to lose him." Morti's voice hitched. "Just like I lost my mother and now I'm losing you girls."

"You're never getting rid of me, even though I'm married now." Zoe reached across the table and squeezed her hand. "I'm still here for you, hon, and I always will be."

"Same. And just because I'm engaged, and a new mother, doesn't mean I don't need you anymore." Tiff slid her hand over Zoe's which was over Morti's. "I need you more than ever, doll."

"Well, you're definitely not losing me." I scoffed, slapping my palm on top of the hand pile. "No one's gonna want this hot mess after the *man attacks*, Voodoo doll, and the Spring Freakshow Festival."

"Thanks, guys." Morti sniffed, then slid her hand out from beneath the pile. "I just feel like I'm falling behind." She looked at Zoe and Tiffany. "You both found everything you were looking for, and you," her gaze slid to mine, "are on the verge of something special, whether you want to admit it or not."

"I don't know what you're talking about." My eyes burned with the desire to look over at Byron.

"I think you do." As if reading my mind, Morti's gaze slid to Byron. I followed suit and saw him watching me when I wasn't looking again. He looked away, and Morti gave me a pointed look. "Your happiness is within your grasp. You just have to be brave enough to reach out and take it."

"What about you?" Zoe chimed in, her brow a puzzle of confusion as she studied Morti. "I thought you were doing the online dating?"

"Online book clubs, remember?"

"Same thing." Tiff waved her hand and sipped her martini. "Your foreplay is discussing plot twists."

"Not these days. With my father's treatments and his spending time with Samantha, I am the one handling everything at the funeral home. He knows I prefer doing the behind-the-scenes requirements. Helping the dearly departed brings me joy. Dealing with the living makes me uncomfortable. That's why I love my book club group. I can be whoever I want to be because no one can see me. It's freeing."

"I'm sure if you tell your father how you feel, he will do something about it." Zoe gave her an encouraging look, ever the optimist.

Morti was already shaking her head. "I don't want to worry him any more than he already is. Prostate cancer might be highly treatable, but it's still cancer. He's going through a lot right now. If I can't help him with his treatments, then I will put my own desires aside and do my damnedest to keep the business running smoothly." She shrugged. "I'm just venting to my besties, is all."

"Speaking of desires, who is that woman hanging all over Studmuffin Storm?" Tiffany squinted to see better.

My head was on a swivel, whipping to the side like a bobblehead, and my jaw fell open. "That is Heather Hunnicut. She is obsessed with good ole PeeWee. What is she doing with *My*ron...I mean Byron?"

"Reaching out and taking it, I'd say." Morti drained the last of her diet cola, studying my reaction.

"Not on my watch." I surged to my feet.

"Oh, boy, this isn't good." Zoe set her drink down.

"Oh, my. What are you going to do, doll?" Tiff dabbed her mouth with a napkin, blinking wide eyes.

"Be brave." I straightened my spine and made a beeline across the pub floor to do something I should have done long ago.

Heather had her hand on Byron's chest, saying something close to his ear. He nodded, his face a neutral mask.

Zander sat across from him with his lips tipped up slightly until he saw me, and then his mouth formed a full-blown grin. Byron finally noticed me, and his eyes widened slightly as he leaned away from Heather.

I didn't stop moving until I came to a stop between his knees, cradled his face in my hands, and planted a kiss square on his lips. Just a short, firm, staking-my-claim kind of kiss. Still...the electricity was breathtaking. I quickly stepped back before Byron could respond and get himself into trouble.

Byron gaped at me.

Heather gasped.

Zanders's lips parted as his eyes narrowed.

I shrugged, secretly thrilled I'd wiped that smug look off his face. "My bad. Clearly, I need more therapy." I grabbed Byron's hand and headed for the door.

"You want to talk about last night?" Byron asked from beneath my car at Jones' Autobody the next morning.

I had dropped him off the night before with no explanation and didn't talk to him again until I called him this morning and asked him to meet me at the garage. My brother, Homer, had agreed to let Byron do the work on my car and use his shop since he had a waiting list of people who wanted him to work on their classic cars.

"What do you mean?" I played dumb. It was easier to sound innocent when he couldn't see my face.

He slid out from beneath my car and raised a honey-brown eyebrow high. He looked delicious in coveralls with his hair pulled back and grease smudged on his cheek. "You kissed me. In public. In front of half the town." He paused a beat. "In front of Judge Jackson." He rolled his body until he stood and leaned against my car, crossing his feet at the ankles and his muscular arms over his chest.

I shook off the distracting sight and thought about his words. "That's exactly why I kissed you, if you want to call it a kiss."

"Your lips pressed against mine." His gaze dropped to my mouth and lingered. "That's a kiss."

"Fine, it was a peck. Judge Jackass looked so smug; I couldn't take it anymore. I wanted to shock the look off his face."

"You succeeded. You also succeeded in making your-self look even more guilty." A rare hint of his frustration was evident in his tone.

"I'm sure he heard my sarcasm when I said, 'Guess I need more therapy.'" Zander knew exactly what he was doing when he had Byron assigned as my sponsor. I was merely letting him know I knew the game he was playing.

"Yeah, well, Zander wasn't the only one watching. I'm not sure anyone else picked up on your sarcasm."

"Anyone as in Heather Hunnicut?" I narrowed my eyes and smirked. Just the mention of that woman's name made my blood pressure rise. Dr. Joy wouldn't be happy with lack of progress in reducing my stress levels.

"Maybe," Byron admitted. "If that kiss was all for

show, then what do you care if I talk to someone else while I'm in town?"

"I don't." I snorted. "If a five-foot nothing plastic Barbie is what you're into, then by all means, talk away, babe."

He studied me with his annoyingly neutral expression. "Sounds like you care more than you're letting on. Is that the real reason you kissed me?"

"No!" I laughed wildly, sounding like a hyena. "I don't care. I mean, I care about you as a friend, and all, but not like 'care' care. You're only in town temporarily." He made me so flustered; I always came off sounding stupid.

"You said you weren't looking for anything serious." He watched me closely. "You just wanted a companion to spend time with so you wouldn't be lonely."

"I said a companion, as in go on dates and be my plus one...not a one-night stand." What was he getting at?

His gaze burned into me, but I couldn't tell what he was thinking. "I can be those things for you."

"Y-You're my therapist." I swallowed hard.

He lifted a shoulder. "I'm also a man."

"Yes, you most certainly are." My words sounded breathy.

His smile came slow and sweet. "Then it's agreed."

I blinked. "W-What did I agree to?"

"Me being your plus one...minus the kissing part, of course." He pointed a knowing finger at me.

Just because I had kissed him, didn't mean I planned to attack him. "So, you *do* believe I'm a sex addict."

"Not what I said." His face was so damned unreadable, it drove me crazy.

I threw up my arms. "Then what are you saying?"

"Everyone needs companionship. It's human nature. I'm happy to be yours if you'll be mine while I'm here. But we must keep things platonic in order for this program to work for you. I think you kissed me because you're attracted to me, and you got jealous when you saw Heather talking to me."

My heart did a flutter. "Well, aren't you full of yourself." I raised my chin a notch. He thought he knew me so well. I mentally groaned. The frustrating part was that he, in fact, actually did.

"Nope. Just stating an observation." He pushed off the car and took a couple steps forward until I could feel his breath on my face.

"Yeah, well here's an observation for *you*." I poked him in the chest. "I think you're just as attracted to me, but you won't let yourself make a move because you're my sponsor, even though you're only doing that because of some debt you feel you owe Zander." I held my breath, surprising myself over my comment.

Electricity filled the silence between us.

He neither confirmed nor denied the observation, leaving me more confused than ever. Instead, he turned toward my car and started working on the floor at the base of the front seats. "Ever think I might be trying to help you catch your rumor spreader?"

I wrinkled my forehead. "What do you mean?"

He rubbed his jaw, looking off in thought. "Heather is territorial of Peter and no fan of yours. Maybe she's spreading the rumors to get Peter's attention and hitting on me because of our connection."

I hadn't thought of it like that. He had a point. "Maybe. I still think Zander is behind it." I had filled him in on everything that had happened in the doctor's office. "The back pain and needle rash are too coincidental if you ask me."

"That's a bit extreme for someone to go to that length to convince the town you're a witch." Byron looked doubtful. "I get Heather might have started the rumors because like everyone else in this small town, I'm sure she heard the Bedazzled Boomer mamas were trying to fix you and Peter up. Heather wanted Peter back, and what better way to do that than sabotage your date? As for Zander being the one to start the rumors, that's a harder sell. What is his motivation?"

"To get back at me." I threw my hands up.

"For what?" Byron studied me quizzically as he ran a hand over the back of his neck as if to ease the tension.

Being my *anything* wasn't an easy job.

"I dumped him in high school after he spread rumors about me being *easy*. His ego couldn't handle it. If he could spread false rumors about me then, I'm sure he's not above spreading rumors about me now."

"I didn't know about that. I'm sorry you had to go through that, especially at such a young age. I'm not excusing what he did back then, but he's a grown man now, not a teenage boy. Maybe he's changed. The man I know wasn't like the boy you describe. Not to mention, he's an honorable man of the law."

"Honorable?" I barked out a laugh. Clearly, we were talking about two different versions of Zander. "That's questionable."

"He took an oath."

"That doesn't mean he's not above breaking it."

I expected him to argue with me, but he didn't, which made me even more curious about what Zander did for Byron to make him so loyal.

"Peter is the one who pressed charges against me. I think Zander saw it as an opportunity to humiliate me by sentencing me to SAA."

"The rumors started before you were arrested."

"Zander hasn't been back in town that long. When he came back and saw I was still here, I think he spread the rumors so no one would want me. He probably hoped if I was lonely and unhappy, then I would leave town and start over somewhere else." I clenched my jaw. "He underestimated me big time."

"I can't say either way on that matter, but do we have a deal?" Byron held out his hand. "I'll be your companion and help you find your rumor spreader, and you stop kissing men...at least until you're through with this program. Think you can handle that?"

"Think *you* can?"

His eyes softened. "I'll try if you try."

I narrowed my eyes, afraid to trust anything good in my life these days. "Why do *you* care so much?"

"We're friends." He shrugged. "I like helping people, and I made a promise." His eyes bore into mine, clear to my soul. "I keep my promises. I'm not leaving until I see this thing through, Harmony, so you might as well accept it."

Oh, I accepted it, all right, but something told me there was more to his story. *What exactly are you hiding, Byron Storm?*

Chapter Twelve

"This would look so nice on you, dear." My mother pulled a floral dress off a rack in *Colonial Couture*, Mayflower's most chic clothing boutique.

"Mother, I am *not* wearing floral prints to anything, let alone Tiffany and Matt's twins' baptism."

"Well, you can't wear jeans. What about something like the dress you wore to my birthday party? You looked lovely in that."

"That wasn't mine. I don't own any dresses, and I'm not buying one to wear for one day." I held up my hand as she started to protest. "Don't worry, I won't wear jeans. I'm sure I can find a decent pair of slacks."

"Oh, honey, your father and brothers are wearing slacks. Can't you find something more...appropriate?"

"For whom, Mother? For you? Dresses are not me. They never have been. I happen to like slacks. Why can't you accept that?" I looked at her, gathering courage to talk to her like Byron had suggested. "Why can't you accept me?"

She blinked and then frowned. "Of course I accept you, darling. What are you saying? You don't think I love you?" Her bottom lip quivered.

"I didn't say that."

"You might as well have." She looked hurt.

"How about this?" I grabbed a one-piece flowy jumpsuit off a rack. "Will this do?" At least it was a solid color—mint green that would make my eyes pop.

Her face brightened, as she blinked away tears and clapped her hands. "Oh, yes. What a lovely compromise. Not a dress, but not slacks, either. It's perfect."

"Cool." I headed to the register.

"Wait...aren't you going to try it on?" She looked at me expectantly.

"No need. It's my size."

Her face fell. "That only took ten minutes."

"My kind of shopping." I grinned until I noticed her disappointment. Groaning internally, I pasted on a smile. "But I'd be happy to help you with yours."

"Wonderful. I was hoping you would say that."

For the next hour, I watched her try on dress after dress, all of them looking the same. It took her forever to make a decision, but we talked the whole time. I had to admit, it was nice catching up on all my siblings, sisters-in-law, and nephews. I liked seeing the genuine smile on her face, knowing I had put it there.

"All set?" I stood.

"Yes. We're going to be the belles of the ball."

"I'm pretty sure the twins will be." I teased.

"Oh, you know what I mean." She led the way to the register. "Wait, what about shoes and a purse? Jewelry?"

"Don't push your luck, Mother." I laughed.

"Okay, honey. I guess I've put you through enough for one day."

"I had fun," I said and realized I actually meant it. We paid for our purchases and headed to the parking lot, where we stopped and stared in disbelief.

My newly fixed, pride and joy tie-dyed Love Bug had been vandalized.

Graffiti with witchcraft symbols and phrases like *go away, leave now, no one wants you, you spell casting sexaholic freak* covered every available inch of the outside of my car. And through a broken window, the door was unlocked with the inside filled with a cauldron, a witch's hat, a broomstick, a book of spells, sex toys, and boxes of condoms in all shapes, sizes, textures, flavors, and colors.

"Oh, my, I feel violated." My mother's hand fluttered to her chest. "Call Officer Pickles and Dr. Joy. I think I'm having a heart attack."

That answered who I took after.

I dialed the phone as I felt my own blood pressure rising. Minutes later, sirens wailed, and the parking lot filled with curious bystanders. Great. Just what I needed. Everything happened in a flurry of chaos.

My mother fainted and was taken to the hospital.

My car became a crime scene and was towed to the police station.

Officer Pickles took my statement.

Father O'Dority held up a crucifix.

Sister Mary Agnes furiously worked her rosary beads.

And my girls finally came to my rescue.

"What happened?" Zoe asked as she drove out of the parking lot with all of us stowed in her minivan.

"I have no clue. Mom and I got our outfits for the baptism, and when we came out of the boutique, my love Bug looked like that." My voice hitched. "That's way more than an April Fool's joke. I'm so mad I could cry." My life was a mess.

"Aww, doll, don't cry." Tiff rubbed my arm. "Things will get better."

"When? I'm so over all this nonsense."

"Do you have any idea who would do something like that?" Morti asked. "Vandalism is a whole different matter than rumors and pranks."

"Rose doesn't like me selling books, and Phoenix doesn't want me to sell antiques. Heather doesn't want me to date Peter, and Peter wants me behind bars. Zander wants me humiliated. Even the mayor gives me a wide berth these days." I sighed. "It literally could be anyone."

"Then that's where we'll start." Zoe turned her minivan around.

"Where are we going?" I asked.

"To the party store. Like you said, it's April, not

Halloween. We need to see who's been making witchy purchases."

"Don't forget all the sex toys and condoms." Tiffany looked as if she were speculating about something. "I wonder if Principal Brimstone can help us with that."

"Why would he?" Morti snorted.

"He's in love and happy instead of miserable these days." Zoe shrugged. "Bitsy accepts him and all his quirks. That goes a long way in changing someone's outlook on life. Maybe he'll be kinder and more helpful than he used to be."

"I suppose it's worth a try to ask," Tiff said. "Maybe we should split up. Divide and conquer, hitting all the avenues, and then report back to each other."

"I'm up for anything because I can't go through another day like today."

"PETER, THERE YOU ARE," I said as I walked through the door of the liquor store, which was right across from my shop.

After my apology lunch at *Lolita's* where he ordered an Old Fashioned, I took a chance that he might be at *Walt's Single Malts* whiskey tasting today. Sure enough he was there, along with half the town. Al was doing a cigar sample since *Shanker's Smoke Shop* was on the outskirts of town and people tended to forget about him.

Peter scanned the bar as his face flushed pink. RJ, Norman, and Sly were there, along with Mack, my father, and several of my brothers. Even Truman was there.

Peter cleared his throat. "Here I am. Though, we already made our peace, so I can't imagine what you want with me now?"

"Hey, my dude, I'm here for the whiskey." I slapped the finely polished oak, twice for good measure. Glancing down the bar, I did a double take.

Phoenix held up her glass and saluted me before she took a sip and sighed as if in great pleasure.

Well, hell. The pressure was on.

Walt poured me a glass of the first whiskey while he went on explaining the flavors. I liked some whiskey but definitely not whiskey and cigars together. The smell of the cigars was making me lightheaded, even with the filtration system. I didn't want Peter getting suspicious and not talking to me, so I tossed back the sample and tried not to wince.

Besides, I couldn't let Phoenix show me up.

Al set an ashtray in front of me with a tiny cigar sample, almost daring me to prove I was a fraud. I picked it up and lit it, taking a puff and trying not to inhale. I nodded my approval and then wheezed just shy of groaning.

"Suit yourself." Peter went back to his own tasting.

Ignoring the curious looks of my father and brothers, who knew darn well I didn't normally imbibe in whiskey or cigars, I leaned in close so only Peter could hear me. "So, did you do anything crazy for April Fools this year?"

He gave me the side eye and sipped his whiskey without a single wince. "No one has done anything crazy since high school."

"Remember when Zander taped all the toilet seats shut in school and our principal peed his pants?"

Peter's lips frowned. "I remember our whole class got in trouble because no one would snitch."

"That's right. We almost didn't get to have Prom." I watched him closely. "I wonder if Zander is still up to his old tricks?"

Peter pushed his glasses up his nose. "I doubt it. We're adults now, Harmony, thank God. I hated high school, and I never went to Prom." He sampled the next whiskey and cigar then eyed me shrewdly.

I sampled my own, looking around for water. "Really? I can't picture you not going to Prom. You're so...so...such a catch."

He choked on his next whiskey sample and stared at me with doubt.

"I mean it," I quickly went on, after sampling my own. I waved the cigar smoke away from my face and blinked my watery eyes. They had ventilation, but clearly it wasn't enough with so many people in attendance. "I bet you could have gone with Heather Hunnicut. You have to know by now that she's had a crush on you since the fifth grade."

His eyes widened. "She's, um, a bit forward."

"And I'm not?" I laughed. "Yet you went on a date with me."

He snorted. "And we see how that turned out."

"Touché."

"Don't you think you've punished yourself enough?" He gave me a knowing look.

"What do you mean?" I swallowed to keep the bile down.

"You're literally green. You're going to get sick if you have any more, so tell me. Why are you really here?"

I thankfully pushed the cigar and whiskey glass away, my head spinning something fierce and my stomach on the verge of rebellion. I took a sip of water. "You've probably heard that my car got vandalized."

He nodded. "Of course I have." His body stiffened as his guard came back up. "You don't think I did that, do you?"

"Not at all," I said and realized I meant it. "We're good, you and me, but I was hoping maybe you might have a clue who it could be?"

He relaxed, his guard coming back down, and he gave my question an honest consideration before shaking his head. "I don't. I really am sorry. I misjudged you. It's one thing for someone to spread rumors that you're a witch—"

"And a sex addict, don't forget that."

"I don't think I could ever forget that," he admitted on a chuckle, "but vandalizing your car is taking things too far. It's over the top. I really don't know why someone is trying that hard to ruin your reputation."

In walked Zander, Byron, Chaz, and Matt.

"Me either, but that's my cue to leave." I stood. "Thanks for talking with me, Peter. I really appreciate it. Excuse me while I go get sick."

"Anytime. Hope you feel better."

I made a beeline past the men whose eyes sprang wide. All except for Byron. His were reduced to slits. No matter how hard I tried, I couldn't get anything by that man. I bolted out the door and headed to my shop just in time.

My apartment was upstairs, but I didn't get that far. I knelt on the bathroom floor, praying to the porcelain god. Strong yet gentle hands touched my back, and I didn't even jump. I somehow knew he would come, even though his friends were across the street. Peeking up, I confirmed what I already knew.

Byron Storm.

I gave him a wobbly smile and then proceeded to get sick again.

I heard the water run. "So, you and Peter, huh?" he said with a soft voice as he rubbed my back and pressed a cold, wet cloth against the back of my neck.

I sighed in pleasure. "Don't stop, babe. That feels so good." I blinked. "Whoops. Sorry. There I go again."

He chuckled. "It's okay. Plenty of women like whiskey and cigars, but clearly you don't. Let me take you to bed."

My mouth fell open. Did I hear him right? "You want to take me to bed? But I thought you said no kissing."

He laughed softly. "I didn't say I would join you. What I meant was you need ginger and sleep."

"Ohhh." Well, shoot, even I heard the disappointment in my voice.

He easily scooped me up into his strong arms, and I settled against his chest, wrapping my arms around his neck. "This is a nice consolation."

He laughed out loud over that one. "I'm happy to oblige." He carried me out of my shop, locked the door behind him, then carried me up the stairs to my apartment and didn't stop until he found my bedroom. "Sit tight while I make you some tea."

I peeled off my jeans and crawled under the covers in just my underwear and t-shirt, still feeling awful.

He returned with a cup of hot ginger and honey tea.

"How did you know I had that?"

"I saw it last time I was here." He handed it to me. "Drink."

I sipped the tea and nodded. "This is good. I'm feeling better already."

He watched me closely. "Why were you there?"

"To get answers."

"Ahhh." He nodded. "I heard about your car."

"I thought maybe Peter might have heard something, but he hasn't." My shoulders slumped, and I sipped my tea.

"Don't worry about your car." He sat on the edge of my bed and patted my leg through the covers, then took the tea from me and set it on the end table. "I'll make sure your Love Bug gets fixed again."

"Thank you." My heavy-lidded eyes fluttered closed.

"Why are you so good to me?" I waited for him to say because it's my job.

"Because you deserve it."

That was the last thing I heard, and I felt his lips press against my forehead before I drifted off to sleep.

Chapter Thirteen

The second week of April, Byron and I agreed to babysit Tiffany and Matt's three-month-old twins at their cute little ranch on the outskirts of town. Her family and Matt's family were getting together with Father O'Dority at Sacred Heart Church to go over everything for the baptism. Zoe had her hands full with her own children's obligations, and Morti was swamped, holding down the fort at the funeral home.

That left one terrified me.

I had oodles of nephews, but no one had trusted me to watch them when they were this little. Byron had two sisters and a few nieces. Since he was a hands-on uncle from the moment they were born, he was a lot more qualified than I was. When he offered to help, I said yes immediately.

The twins were napping at the moment, thank you universe.

"Tiffany's twin sister, Tabatha, and Matt's cousin, Finn, are the godparents." I sat on the living room sofa, making conversation because I didn't know what else to do. Tiff's place was spotless, and she had already sterilized and filled the babies' bottles in the fridge.

"Finn's a good ten years younger than Tabatha, but it's evident to everyone that he fancies her." Byron winked, two cushions down from me.

"Tiff said there's a definite spark between them. I hope they work out. Tabatha deserves happiness after all she's been through." I held my breath as I heard the babies stirring in their cribs through the monitor, but then they settled once more. I exhaled slowly, much to Byron's amusement, before continuing in a softer voice so as not to disturb them. "Her husband and daughter died in a house fire years ago, and she never moved on. After reconnecting with Tiffany and her twins, Tabatha finally seems ready to let someone in."

"According to Matt, Finn hasn't had it easy, either. His fiancée cheated on him with his best friend one day before their wedding. That's why he packed his bags and came to America to help his uncle out. I don't think he's dated since."

"They sound like a perfect match." I stared off dreamily. That's all I wanted. To find my person and share life with them.

"You would be surprised the kind of people who end up being a perfect match." Byron's words broke the spell I was under. Actually, the tone of his words. For someone who said I couldn't kiss him again, his tone and the look in his eyes said otherwise.

"I would?" My gaze dropped to his lips, and I couldn't help leaning slightly forward. To my surprise, he did, too.

The twins started wailing, and we both jerked apart before we crossed a line. Yes, I had kissed him before, but that was all for show for Zander's sake. If we kissed again, it wouldn't be ethical...would it? I had to get through the program before anything more could happen between us.

But after I was through with the program, he would return to his life in Boston, which was about an hour away from Connecticut, so what was the point? I didn't want long distance, and he hadn't expressed that he even wanted me, period.

The twins wailed louder.

"We'd better go." He stood and held out a hand.

I slid mine into his, ignoring the tingle that was always there whenever we touched, and allowed him to help me to my feet. I dropped his hand immediately and followed several feet behind, not trusting myself to touch him.

All thoughts of romance fled as we entered the nursery. The twins were big at birth with Matt McGinnis as their father, but they still looked so tiny to me. The only time I had held my nephews as infants was sitting down with my mother hovering over me. I didn't babysit any of them until they were over one year old and could walk.

I rubbed my palms on my jeans and bit my bottom lip before looking up at Matt, helplessly. "What do I do?"

"Pick her up. She won't break." He gestured to Genie as he picked up Declan as if he'd done so a thousand times.

Genie was the spitting image of Tiffany's Granny, Eugenia Eisenhower, and just as feisty. Declan had Matt's agreeable looks and disposition. "How come I get the fussy one?" I was terrified of breaking her.

"You'll be fine. Just put one hand behind her head and the other under her back and bottom then lift her to your chest."

I did as he instructed, holding my breath until she was in my arms, then sighing my relief. Sliding her into the crook of my arm, I stared at her little heart-shaped face and melted. She looked up at me with teary blue eyes, and I fell head over heels in love as my own eyes grew misty.

"You're not so bad when you don't scream, little one." She sniffled and her breath hitched, her eyes mesmerized by mine as if she'd found a kindred spirit. "I know. Life can be hard, but don't you worry, babe. Auntie Harm has got you." I looked up and caught Byron staring at me with the oddest expression.

He blinked and his face turned into a neutral mask again. "You're actually a natural. Who knew?"

"Tiff knew." I tilted my head. Leave it to my best friend to know me better than I knew myself. "That's why she trusted her precious babies to me."

"To us." He nodded once.

"True, so let's feed these wee little ones, Uncle Byron. They must be starving if they're anything like their daddy."

"Not so fast, Auntie Harm. First, we change their diapers. I'm sure they're wet after their nap."

"Good point." We set the babies on their changing tables, and I followed everything he did. "I don't know why my family never trusted me to do this before." I picked Genie up and her diaper, that was clearly on backwards, proceeded to fall off.

Byron laughed. "Gee, I can't imagine why." He held Declan out to me. "Here, let's switch and I'll—"

"Not a chance, dude. I've got my girl. You take that Sasquatch to the kitchen and heat up those bottles. I'll be out in a jiffy."

"Come on, little buddy. You might as well learn now that it's best not to argue with a fiery redhead."

"Exactly." I watched them disappear and then proceeded to put a new diaper on Genie the correct way, pleased as punch when it worked. "And you, my little princess, need to learn to stand up for yourself right away."

Genie's face scrunched up, and she let out an ear-piercing wail.

I barked out a laugh. "Good girl! Well, alrighty then. Let's go eat."

Over the next hour, we fed the twins, burped them, changed diapers that were far more than just wet this time, changed outfits that had spit up on them, rocked the babies, and put them back down for another nap.

I'd never been more exhausted in my life.

"I don't know how Tiffany and Matt do this every

day?" I sat at the kitchen table with a sigh, not trusting the sofa again.

"Babies are a lot of work." Byron made a pot of coffee and brought me a cup, with *no* cream and sugar. "Yes, I remembered." He chuckled.

"Thanks." I took a grateful sip. "I've never felt the want or need to have children." I peeked over at him as he sat across from me. "How about you?"

He shrugged. "Same," he said, surprising me. That could be a deal breaker if one person wanted children, and the other one didn't. "Don't get me wrong, I love my nieces, but I get to spoil them and then leave when I want to."

"Right? My nephews are awesome dudes, but I get to choose when I want to hang out with them. If I want to travel or go out, there's nothing stopping me."

"How's your mother feel about that?"

"She ignores me when I talk like that, thinking I'll change my mind if I find the right man. That's not going to happen."

"If you find the right man, maybe he'll feel the same way as you, and then it won't be an issue."

"That's the plan, but easier said than done, my man." I looked him in the eyes. "Got any single friends?"

That gave him pause for a minute, and I could have sworn he looked jealous. "You can't date, remember?"

I shrugged. "I mean for when I make it through this program."

His gaze refused to let mine go. "And when you make

it through this program, I think I know a guy who might be perfect for you."

I swallowed hard, my throat suddenly dry. "You do, huh?" I sucked in a little breath before asking, "Anyone I know...?"

Once again, we were saved by the bell when Tiffany and Matt got home.

"I HAVE no idea what to get Genie and Declan." I browsed the shelves of *Mayflower Munchkins* with Zoe and Morti. "What are you guys getting them?"

"They certainly don't need clothes. I swear I don't think those babies have worn a single outfit twice. Tiff can't seem to help herself when it comes to fashion." Zoe shook her head on a chuckle.

"Very true," I seconded, adding, "I know Matt's family has sent a ton of boxes over from Ireland."

"Her mother and sister stop by almost daily with something new as well." Morti snorted. "Must be nice to have that kind of support system. If I ever have children, it's me and my dad, and that's pretty much it."

"Don't forget about the father's family." Zoe smiled, ever the optimist.

"Let's be realistic. Mine will most likely come from a sperm bank." Morti had always been a pessimist, but lately, she was worse than normal.

"I bet you will find someone when you're not looking,

Morti. That's usually how it happens. And if you don't, then you will rock being a single mom because you have us." I tended to fall somewhere in the middle.

Tiff was a die-hard realist, but even she had softened since having her babies.

"I definitely don't know what I would do without you girls." Morti held up a cross. "What about this? It has a little prayer on it."

"That's precious." Zoe walked over to another shelf. "This is cute, too." She held up a plaque with a saying about getting baptized."

"That's perfect," Morti said.

"That still leaves me." I sighed. "I don't want to get anything controversial from my shop because I don't need any more drama in my life." I spotted a picture frame. "What about this? I can have it engraved with their names and the date, and Tiff can put a picture of the twins with their godparents in it."

"Speaking of godparents, did you guys hear that Finn asked Tabatha on a date?" Zoe's eyes filled with stars. She was a sucker for love.

"I heard he took her to that fancy new restaurant in Liberty." Morti frowned. "I don't blame him for choosing another town. This town is far too nosy."

"Amen to that, sister." Zoe made her way to the register.

We all paid for our gifts and headed outside.

"I don't have to be back at the funeral home for another hour." Morti looked at her watch. "Want to get coffee?"

"Sure, I have time. I don't have to relieve my brother at my shop for a bit, and I can always go for coffee."

"That works for me. I have a meeting with Matt and Tiffany to go over the last-minute details for the baptismal party next week." They'd chosen to use the church's parish center."

"Cool." Morti led the way across the street to *Pilgrim Perks Café.*

We ordered our coffee and pastries to go along with it, then sat down with our goods.

"A little birdie told me you were a pro with the twins." Zoe bit into a scone and sipped her tea.

"I surprised myself, but I couldn't have done it without Byron." I blew on my coffee with cream and sugar then popped a donut hole in my mouth.

"Speaking of your hunky sponsor...how is Studmuffin Storm?" Morti sipped her black coffee and nibbled on a bran muffin.

"Confusing," I admitted.

"How so?" Zoe puckered her brow.

I told them about our conversation while babysitting the twins. "He tells me no kissing is allowed, and we have to keep things strictly professional. Then he comes to my aid when I get sick from the cigar and whiskey, then he offers to help me babysit and proceeds to flirt with me and talk about the perfect guy for me, hinting it might be him. He's so hard to read, it's driving me crazy."

"We all know you don't really need SAA, and he's only your sponsor because he owes Zander a favor. If you two got together, he wouldn't be doing you any real harm. And while he's offered you some advice, you haven't actually paid him for his services, therefore he's not actually your therapist. You're both adults and free to do what you want. I say go for it. Screw Zander. It's clear you and Byron have chemistry. By denying that, you might be missing out on something special. Trust me, it's not that easy to meet a good man."

"Oh, trust me, I agree. I'm just not so sure Byron actually wants me, and I'm not looking for another short-term affair. I'm over that. I want a companion. A partner to share life with, and unfortunately, his life is in Boston and mine is here."

"Long distance isn't impossible. A lot of people do that." Zoe smiled encouragingly. "Maybe you should talk to him."

"I just don't want to get my hopes up and then get my heart broken." I groaned. "Why does he have to be exactly my type?"

"Because Zander is good and knew exactly what he was doing when he paired you two together." Morti's face twisted in anger.

"He sure did. Byron is such a good listener, and he thinks my quirks are funny. He sees right through my bull-shit and doesn't let me get away with it. He knows when I'm trying to be cool to cover up how I'm really feeling. He *gets* me."

"That's so rare, hon." Zoe squeezed my hand. "Are you sure you want to let that slip away from you?"

"I'm not sure of anything."

"I know you might not want to hear this, but maybe the person you need to talk to is Zander." Morti shrugged one shoulder.

"Why? What purpose would that possibly serve?" I didn't want to be anywhere near Zander because I was afraid of what might come out of my mouth.

"To finally make peace and possibly get your sentence reduced to time served." Morti held up her hands. "Maybe he'll let you out of the program early."

"That's not a bad idea." Zoe nodded. "At the very least, maybe you will find out why Byron owes Zander a favor."

"Okay, Okay. I'm warming up to the idea. And maybe I'll even find evidence proving Zander is the one who started the rumors in the first place."

Chapter Fourteen

I sat with my family for Easter Sunday service at Sacred Heart Church. All my brothers, sisters-in-law, and nephews were there. They might blow off the occasional brunch, but they all knew better than to miss a holiday with our mother.

We took up three entire pews!

We didn't even have to get there early to sit together. Everyone loved my mother and left the first three rows on the left side empty for every holiday. In the center front rows sat Tiffany, Matt, her parents and sister. His cousins, uncle, and other siblings as well as his parents had made the trip from Ireland because the twins were getting baptized during mass after the homily. On the right side, front and center, sat Morticia, her father and Samantha, with Zoe, Chaz, her children, her parents, her ex-in-laws, and Chaz's parents.

Byron had gone back to Boston for the holiday to be

with his family. I'd felt off since the day he left. Even though I was surrounded by a loving family, I felt empty and alone. I didn't understand it. Yes, I'd been lonely before and longing for companionship, but I'd never felt quite like this.

Like a piece of me was missing.

"Honey, are you okay?" My mother touched my arm.

I flinched. "Sorry. Yes, I'm fine." My father had always been the one to give bear hugs and kisses. I knew my mother loved me, but she didn't express it in the normal motherly ways. She wanted to teach me etiquette and manners, then dress me up like a doll and show me off. She didn't like things messy, and since I was messy most of the time, she didn't give hugs.

I suddenly realized maybe that was why I was a tomboy. I'd never felt good enough for my mother, so why try? If I acted like the boys, I got plenty of attention from my father, and that was all I'd needed.

Or so I'd thought...

It had taken forty years to realize I needed my mother, too.

I reached out and grabbed her hand, startling her. "Sorry...I just...it's a holiday, and all, you know?" I started to let go of her hand, but she gripped mine tighter and smiled up at me with misty eyes. Maybe Byron was right. Maybe I needed to talk to my mother.

Maybe just maybe, my mother needed me, too.

The homily ended and Matt, Tiffany, the twins, Tabatha, and Finn went up on the altar. Father O'Dority performed the baptism, and there wasn't a dry eye in the room. They really were such angels. When mass was over, everyone went outside for pictures and then headed next door to the parish center, where the celebration continued.

"Even without a baptism, your babies are angels, Tiff." I stared at Tabatha holding Genie and Finn holding Declan as they talked to Matt and his parents.

"They really are, aren't they." Tiffany beamed with pride and love, staring at her babies and their daddy.

"I have to say Tabatha and Finn look good together." Zoe studied them with a small smile on her lips.

"Matt says he really likes her, and she seems to be so much happier these days. I have high hopes they work out. All I want is for her to be as happy as I am. I'm sure holding my babies is hard on her after losing her own, but she never lets on. She and my mother have both become so important to me. And I've finally made my peace with Grammy for keeping them from me."

"That's good." Morti nodded. "It's important to make amends before it's too late. Life goes by so quickly. I never really gave that much thought, but it's so true."

"How's your father, Morti?" I squeezed her shoulder.

"The chemo has been harder on him than we expected, but he's hanging in there. I have to admit Samantha has been very good to him."

"Good," Zoe said gently, giving her a hug. "That's one less thing for you to worry about."

"I suppose." Morti looked around the room, changing

the subject. "Nice turnout, Tiff. And great job as usual with the decorations, Zoe."

"Thanks." Zoe smiled.

"I think this town has finally warmed up to me since I've done so much with Grammy's money, and well, they love Matt, so that helps." Tiffany laughed and then studied me. "That jumpsuit looks fantastic on you, Harmony. I love that pale shade of green like your eyes." Tiffany hugged me. She wore a chic robin's egg blue pencil skirt with a cotton candy pink silk blouse tucked in, already back to her old size with slightly more curves that looked healthy and great on her.

"Why, thank you." I spun around in a dramatic circle, feeling pretty. Feminine. I blinked. Good grief, my mother just might be on to something about the whole dressing up thing, though I would never admit that to her or she'd have me in a dress every day.

"Too bad Studmuffin Storm isn't here to see it." Zoe winked, looking lovely in a flowy yellow sundress with tiny white daisies all over it.

Morti frowned, looking serious like she normally did in her grey and black suit with her hair pulled back in its standard low bun. "No, but someone else is here."

I followed her gaze and saw Zander across the room, talking to Tiffany's lawyers, Victoria Steele and Alexandra Knight of the Steely Knight Agency.

"That's weird. I didn't invite him." Tiff's face puckered in confusion. "Maybe he stopped in to discuss a case with them or something."

"Whatever the reason, this might be your chance to talk to him, Harm." Zoe nudged me in his direction. "What are you waiting for?"

Taking a deep breath, I headed across the room just as Zander walked out the door. I hurried outside and caught up with him.

"Zander, wait." I wrapped my arms around my ribs, forgetting my coat. The third week of April was still chilly in Massachusetts. "Can I speak with you for a minute?"

He stopped and slowly turned around, looking me up and down with a raised eyebrow. "Ms. Jones, to what do I owe this...well, I would say pleasure, but we both know that it's not. What can I do for you?" He glanced at his watch. "Your minute starts now."

I ground my teeth but didn't take the bait. "I saw you in there talking to Tiffany's lawyers, and it reminded me you're a judge. Who do you think is spreading the rumors about me? Clearly you don't believe I am a witch casting spells anymore, after the vandalism to my car."

He rubbed his back. "I don't know what I believe, Ms. Jones."

"Seriously, Zander, don't you think we're beyond formalities? We've slept together, for crying out loud."

"That was a long time ago." His jaw hardened.

"Exactly." I put my hands on my hips. "You're a grown man. Why are you still holding a grudge about something that happened when we were young and stupid?"

"You humiliated me."

"Ditto, babe." I threw up my hands. "You made everyone believe I was some sex starved maniac."

"I do believe you're serving a sentence for that very thing." His voice oozed with sarcasm.

"Dammit, Zander, you and I only slept together once, and it wasn't very good, but I didn't tell anyone." I lowered my voice when people looked our way. "I would have given you another chance if you hadn't gone around bragging as if we'd done it a hundred times. That really hurt me, you know."

His face flushed. "Like you said, we were young and stupid."

"Well, we're not now, but this sentence is stupid."

He let out a long sigh. "Harmony, I know what you think, but it's not true. I didn't sentence you to SAA to punish you for the past. Your actions toward several men in town were a bit excessive. They're the ones who pressed charges. I can't dismiss that, and I gave you a choice. I can't help it your family intervened."

"Okay, I get it. Your hands were tied. I was desperate for someone, *anyone*, to take me seriously. But I tell you, someone is trying to ruin my life by spreading those rumors, and ransacking my car is taking things too far."

"I agree," he said without hesitation.

I blinked. "You do?"

"Yes." He nodded, and his jaw hardened. "I am doing everything I can to find out who it is."

"Good, then you agree I shouldn't have to complete SAA?"

"No," he said firmly. "You might not be a sex addict, but you clearly have issues you need to work out."

"And you just happen to interfere by assigning Byron Storm as my sponsor?" I scoffed. "You know he's my type, which tells me you're setting me up to fail."

This time *he* blinked. "Now how in the world would I know he's your type? You and I dated, and Byron and I don't exactly look alike."

He had a point. I chewed my bottom lip, wondering if I had misjudged the entire situation. "Then why did you assign him to me?"

"Because he's the best, Harmony." Zander's voice rang with sincerity. "Contrary to what you might think, I'm not a bad guy. I felt guilty for how I treated you when we were kids and have always wanted to make it up to you."

"By sending me to SAA?" I laughed, but it didn't have much bite to it this time.

"I had to satisfy the town, but I also wanted you to get some help with whatever issues you clearly have. Byron owed me a favor, so I called him in on it."

"And what exactly did you do for him?"

"That's on a need-to-know basis, and you don't need to know." His eyes narrowed. "Clearly, I made a poor judgment if I put too much temptation in front of you. I can have him removed if you think it's too—"

"No! I mean, no, that's okay. Byron has actually been helping me a lot. I know, I know. I am definitely not a sex addict, and I would never have admitted this before now, but you're right. I do have a few things I need to work through, and Byron's been helping me with that. How did you know he was the best?"

Zander's eyes met mine and held. "Because he helped me."

LATER THAT EVENING, I left my mother's house after Easter dinner and headed back home. It felt so good to have my car back. My brother had pity on me—after I complained to our mother, of course—and bumped me ahead of his regular customers to replace the window, especially since Byron was out of town.

Parking my car out back, I slipped into the back room of my shop because I forgot to check on the inventory of my witchcraft supplies. There had been a sudden uptick of people who were fascinated with the spiritual belief system much to my mother's dismay.

Ever since the rumors of me being a crazy spell-casting witch had started, I had been talking more and more about witchcraft and psychic mediums with my customers. The people in town—whether out of fear or curiosity—wanted to know more. People wanted books on the subject, as well as sacred objects, central to the practice of witchcraft, so they could focus on keeping a balance and harmony in life.

My business had increased substantially.

I wanted to place an order tonight, so I needed to check on a couple things I forgot. I came in through the back door and was perusing every supply shelf, when suddenly, I heard a noise out in the front of my shop. It was dark outside, and my shop was closed.

Who could it be?

Glancing around, I spotted the only thing I could see that I could use as a weapon...a broomstick. I rolled my eyes and groaned. This could only happen to me. Holding the broom like a bat, I crept to the door and slowly turned the knob.

I froze and listened.

Silence.

Just when I thought I was going crazy and that no one was there, I heard footsteps. Creeping out of the room, I stayed in a crouched position and walked quietly on my toes with my broomstick raised and ready. I followed the sound of the footsteps to the center of the room. I saw a shadow with its hood up, bending over my counter.

I didn't hesitate.

I swung my broomstick hard.

I heard a resounding thunk, followed by a scream...a high-pitched scream. Jogging over to the wall, I flicked on the lights. A body was curled up on the floor, whimpering with its head covered by a hood.

I held my broomstick ready. "Who are you, and why are you in my shop?"

The person sat up, and their hood fell away.

I gaped. "Heather?"

"Why'd you hit me? I should have you arrested." She stood.

The audacity of this woman astounded me. "Arrest me? For what? You are the one who broke into my store."

Her eyes widened over my broom. "For dark magic. I knew you were a witch. Oh my God if you turn my hair into snakes, I'll cry. I'm too pretty for that."

"You're too dumb for that. Wrong religion. Medusa was a part of Greek mythology." *Good grief, this town is killing me.* "What the hell are you doing in my shop this late, Heather, and don't lie to me." I shook my broom. "I'll know."

Her face registered guilt. "I admit, I was shopping in here when I knew you weren't around. Your brother was manning the store."

"Okay, but why come back after it closed?"

"I think I left my wallet here." She looked sheepish.

"You have to admit you look shady with your hood up."

"I just happen to be wearing a hoodie. I knocked on the door, but you were closed, then I tried the doorknob out of curiosity. I can't help that whoever closed up left the door unlocked. I thought maybe someone was here, so I came in and called out. I freaked out for a moment when I realized no one was here, so I put my hood up and thought I would at least peek and see if my wallet was behind the counter."

I must have arrived after she was already inside because I hadn't heard a thing, and I did come in through the back. "And was it?"

"Not that I can see."

Could this day get any stranger? "You really expect me to believe that you came to my store to shop?"

She shrugged. "You really do have the best oils, and I wanted to see if you had a love potion to make Peter know that I exist."

"You don't need a love potion. Peter definitely knows you exist; he's just terrified of you."

"Me?" She looked genuinely shocked. "Why on earth would he be afraid of little ole' me?"

"Because you're a princess, and he's a frog. A man like Peter has no idea what to do with a woman like you."

Her eyes widened. "But he wasn't intimidated by you?"

"I'm no princess."

"Are you kidding me? Have you looked in the mirror? You really have no idea how beautiful you are." She looked at me in disbelief.

I eyed her doubtfully. "I am not girly whatsoever."

"No, you're not." She shook her head in confusion. "What does that have to do with being pretty?"

This time I was shocked. "Wow, I guess it doesn't." I'd never really thought about that. My mother had me so convinced that not being classically pretty was unattractive.

"You're edgy and exciting and badass. You seriously could have any man you want if you would stop coming on so strong and pushing them away."

Byron was right. I really did need to sit down and have a heart-to-heart with my mother, and I never thought I would say this in a million years, but I was actually grateful to Zander. If he hadn't given me this sentence, then I would never have realized I might not need sex therapy, but I definitely needed someone to help me confront my issues.

"Thank you, Heather." Another thing I never thought I would hear myself say.

She laughed at that. "I broke into your shop...sort of... and you're thanking me? I should thank you for making me realize I was approaching Peter in the wrong way. But...are you sure you don't have a thing for him? He's quite the catch."

"Oh, I'm sure. Peter's a good egg," I said and realized I meant it, "but he's not my type. He'd be lucky to have you. I have someone else in mind for me, but I'm not sure he's into me, either."

"Then maybe you're going about things the wrong way, too."

Chapter Fifteen

"And how is everyone today?" Dr. Hastings said, her pure white, short hair was slicked back behind her ears as usual, and her faded blue eyes stared us down knowingly, like she could see clear into our souls.

"Great."

"Good."

"So much better."

We all chorused. Again, it was just the six of us, but we were all from small towns, so it wasn't that surprising that our 12-step program was smaller than other types.

"As I knew you would be." She winked. "This process is a success if you stay open and put in the work. By now you should have admitted you were powerless over your addictive sexual behavior. You wouldn't be here if your lives hadn't become unmanageable."

"Um, yeah, it was seriously hard to manage that many men and remember all of my cheer routines not to mention pass my classes." Misty Davenport shook her head, her high bottle-blonde ponytail swaying. Amber eyes looked at me innocently. "Right, Harmony?"

"As hard as remembering all of my brother's names." I shrugged. "I just don't know how I managed."

"And how is it going, allowing a higher power to restore your sanity? I take it you've turned your life over and made a moral inventory of yourself? Have you admitted to your God, yourself and another human being, like maybe your sponsor, the exact nature of your wrongs?" Shirley stared into me as if she were on to me and expected me to drop the games and tell her the truth.

I swallowed hard; my mouth suddenly dry. I thought about her questions. Yes, I believed in a higher power. I always had. I just didn't put a name to her. And I definitely sought help with the current mess I was in, and if I were being honest, with discovering the reasons behind the issues I was discovering I had.

I nodded. "It's going well. I've learned a lot about myself lately. Due in part to making amends with people and getting insightful advice in places I hadn't expected."

"Isn't it wonderful when the happens? Thank you for sharing, Harmony." Shirley looked at the elderly man beside Misty. "Bernard, have you humbly asked your God to remove your shortcomings and defects of your character?"

"Hi, Shirley." Bernie smoothed his thick head of silver hair back and his gray eyes sparkled. "I have indeed, and I feel like a new man. So much lighter. Free."

"And how does your lady friend feel about that?" Shirley tilted her head, studying him, taking notes.

"She's happy with my progress. I'm not out of the doghouse yet, so to speak, but I'm getting there."

"Good for you. Thank you for sharing, Bernie." Shirley nodded. "I have faith you'll get there." She looked at the elderly woman beside Misty. "And how about you, Mae? Have you made amends with your husband?"

"I have, and it feels wonderful. We're both learning to compromise. It's done wonders for our marriage to be open and honest. I'm a lot more satisfied and at peace these days." The petite woman adjusted her small round glasses that hung on a chain around her neck, then tilted her black and gray hair in a low bun until it was straight.

"That's half the battle. Keep at it, Mae. The rewards far exceed the journey." Shirley looked at a young man in his thirties. "And how about you, Lorenzo? Have you learned to admit when you're wrong and continue to pray and meditate?"

"I sure did. My uncle let me keep my job as night watchman of the museum, and I leave my device at home now. I actually bring a book to read. It helps keep my mind centered." He laughed. "Who knew I would become a reader?"

"Reading can be very therapeutic. Thanks for sharing." Shirley smiled and looked at the last man. "How about you, Duke? Have you had a spiritual awakening? Are you ready to practice these principles in your everyday life and help others in need?"

The bald, muscular man puffed out his chest. "Yo, Doc, I am a pillar of respect to the ladies these days. My mama is the one trying to fix me up now, telling anyone who will listen what a gentleman I am. Can you believe it? But no worries, I'm all work and no play...until closing time, capiche?" He winked and let out a booming laugh.

"You're doing good work, but I think you're missing the point a little bit, Duke. Don't let addictive behavior of any kind rule your life whether you're open or closed. Human beings are complex, interesting, wonderful creatures that are about so much more than sex. Don't dwell on the physical so much. Try to explore the intellectual aspect of the people in your life. Can you try to do that for me?"

"You mean no sex at all?" He gaped at her. "I thought you just meant during working hours."

"Sex can be a wonderful experience if done for the right reasons and not used as a crutch to block out other emotions you might be going through. It's no different than any other addiction. Before giving into your urges, think about why you want to have sex first."

"I'll try, but I'm not gonna lie. That's going to be hard."

"Breaking an addiction is hard." Shirley looked around the room one last time. "You're all making wonderful progress and so close to conquering the power of this disease that has so much control over you. Just remember, while you might tame the beast, it will always be there, lurking in the shadows, ready to take control again if given the chance. Be vigilant. Be strong. Don't let it consume you. Fall back on the things that work for you and reach out to your sponsors." Her gaze landed on me. "They are there to help you day or night."

And that right there was the problem.

"Here you go." I handed Gerty and Gabby Rogers their bag with everything they would need to set up their altar. "Remember, the instructions are inside. Just keep an open mind and focus on the outcome you wish to experience."

"This is all so exciting." Gerty clapped her hands.

One minute I was a scary witch, and now suddenly everyone wanted my advice. I offered to help, but they insisted they wanted to be their own witches as if it were a party game. Who was I to argue with that? As long as they weren't using what I gave them for evil to harm others, then I was fine with it. It didn't hurt that I was at an all-time high financially as well.

"It can be. Follow my instructions and choose what works best for you. There are a lot of spirits, even ones who are fierce and protective mother figures, that invoke financial stability and protect one's resources."

"I just love that there are strong and independent ones like us." Gabby rubbed her hands together. "If Harmony can overcome obstacles, then so can we, sister."

"That's right, Gabby." Gerty clapped her hands this time. "We're going to have so much fun with our cute little altar. And I have the perfect spot for it."

"Who says you get to pick the spot?" Gabby took the

bag from Gerty as they walked out the door, arguing every step of the way.

I closed my eyes and rubbed my temples.

The door chimed again, and I groaned.

"What did you for—" I sucked in a breath. "You're here."

Byron Storm stood before me in the flesh, looking mouth-watering good in a pair of tight jeans and a black heavy metal rock band t-shirt. He'd been gone a week instead of just a weekend, and I had begun to wonder if he wasn't coming back.

"I'm here. Did you miss me?" He laughed.

I felt my face flush. Could he read my mind so well? "I, um, er..."

"I missed you, too, buddy." He winked.

"Oh, yeah, right. Me, too." I shrugged.

And just like that I was back in the friend zone.

"So, what did I miss while I was gone?"

"Lots." I laughed. "Let me lock up and I'll fill you in upstairs."

His smiled slipped a little.

"For coffee?"

He nodded, and then followed me up the stairs.

"The baptism was perfect." I talked as I made a pot of coffee. "Babies aren't my thing, but those twins are the exception. They really are angels. I plan to be the cool auntie once they are toddlers, but Finn and Tabatha looked right at home holding them."

"Maybe they'll be the next lucky couple."

"Maybe. They look really good together." I held up a bottle of Irish whiskey and arched a brow at him. A little of the fruity, smooth whiskey I could do. Harsh whiskey with a bite to it and cigars...not so much.

"Sure, why not?"

I added the shot and handed him a cup, then brought the pot and the bottle over to the table. Pouring a cup for myself, I added a shot to my own and picked up where I had left off. "Let's see, what else." I blew over the rim of my cup and then took a sip. Damn that tasted good. "I had a moment with my mother at the baptism."

"You did?" He looked surprised.

"Yeah. It was a brief moment. I grabbed her hand, and she didn't let go. It sounds stupid, now that I said it out loud." I looked away.

"That doesn't sound stupid at all."

"My mother has never been big on physical touch. I needed that."

"I'm proud of you." His voice softened. "Taking a chance takes courage."

"Better late than never, I guess," I cleared my throat, "but I think you're right."

"Excuse me?" He slapped a hand over his chest. "Care to say that again?"

"Very funny," I laughed, "but in all honesty, I think I need to talk to her. Like really talk to her."

"Good for you." He nodded, his face transforming into one of pride. "What made you change your mind?"

"Not what...who." I shook my head, realizing a lot *had*

happened when he was gone. "Heather Hunnicut broke into my shop."

He choked on his coffee. "Wait...did I just hear you right? Heather? What happened? Did you call the police?"

"No." I chuckled because I still couldn't believe everything that had gone down. "I hit her over the head with a broomstick."

"You did not." His face looked comical.

"I did." I couldn't help the giggle that slipped out.

He laughed in spite of himself. "Why did she break in?"

"Technically she didn't break in. Harry was the last one to close up, and he forgot to lock the door. That doesn't surprise me one bit because he's done it before."

"Yikes." Byron refilled his cup and added another shot, then topped mine off as well before setting the pot back down.

"Yeah. Anyway, she says she shops in my store when I'm not around. She thought she left her wallet behind, so she went back. The door was unlocked, so she thought Harry was still there. He wasn't, but since she was already inside, she peeked behind my counter."

"How did you catch her? Security alarms?"

"Actually, that's another thing that's broken that I haven't gotten around to fixing yet." Owning your own business involves a constant to-do list.

"I can help with that, too, if you'd like."

I eyed him with a raised eyebrow. "What are you, a jack of all trades?"

"Guilty, and believe me, I'm a master of none." His lips quirked into a half-smile. "I just tinker."

"Well, then I might take you up on that offer as well."

"Good, now back to Heather. So, if not because of your security system, how did you catch her?"

"I had come in through the back to check my inventory since I was placing an order for more witchcraft supplies," I saw the look on his face and clarified, "apparently, I'm all the rage. The rumor spreader tried to ruin me, yet ironically, people are more fascinated than ever. Business is booming."

"Well, that's a silver lining if ever I've seen one."

"I'm not complaining, but back to Heather. I actually believe she's telling the truth. I learned a thing or two about myself."

"Yeah? That's great." I could see the curiosity in his heavy-lidded eyes. He looked as relaxed as I felt. Right from the start there had been a level of comfort between us that I'd never had with anyone else.

I took another sip of my spiked coffee, the whiskey warming its way down my insides deliciously. "I never put much stock into my looks, knowing I wasn't classically pretty like my mother, no matter how hard she tried to make me. There is a reason the men in town run the other way when I come near. I never imagined my uniqueness in itself could be that appealing. Heather made me realize men are intimidated by me because of my actions, and not my looks. So maybe I am my own worst enemy."

"Which is exactly what I've been saying." He carried

his cup to the sink, and I followed him with my own. "You don't need to put on a show for people to see you, Harmony Jones. You're beautiful both inside and out, just the way you are."

I had waited so long to hear someone say those words, tears filled my eyes. What was wrong with me? I reached up to swipe them away. His hand snagged mine and his thumb gently brushed a tear off my cheek. We stood a breath apart, searching each other's eyes. I didn't think, I just reacted, throwing myself against him and pressing my lips to his.

He paused, but when I slipped my tongue between his lips to touch his, he snapped and angled his head, deepening the kiss. He spun our bodies around and leaned his body against mine, so I was pinned to the counter, wrapping his arms around me and holding me tight while he devoured my mouth.

I couldn't think, couldn't catch my breath, couldn't do anything but lose myself in the moment. I'd never been kissed like this or felt a more powerful connection. I ran my hands over his face and hair and body, needing to feel all of him at once. When I lifted my legs and wrapped them around his waist, he ground against me, his hands sliding beneath my ass to squeeze me then one hand slid up beneath my t-shirt and cupped my breast.

My head fell back, and I moaned.

His hand stilled.

I felt the shift, and my body grew cool as he pulled my shirt back down and set me on my feet, then took a step away. "I'm so sorry. I crossed the line." His gaze met mine and filled with regret.

That hurt the worst.

"I kissed you, remember?" I raised my chin a notch.

"I kissed you back, and...more." He slowly shook his head, looking disgusted with himself. "I'm your therapist."

"You're my sponsor. I never actually hired you as my therapist." I crossed my arms over my middle. "No worries, Doc. We just got caught up in the heat of the moment. It won't happen again."

He reached out to touch me. "Harmony, I—"

"I talked to Zander," I blurted as I stepped out of reach.

Byron's hand paused. "What did you guys talk about?"

If I didn't know better, I would swear he was nervous. "Why he pulled strings to get you as my sponsor. He said you're the best, and that you helped him a long time ago, and that's all he wanted for me."

Byron looked guarded. "Zander is far from perfect, but he is no longer the bad guy you think he is." His gaze locked onto mine. "Did he say anything else?"

I stared him down. "He didn't tell me your secret if that's what you mean."

Tension filled the air between us.

"It's getting late," he finally said. "I should get home. I haven't even unpacked. I just wanted to check in to see how you were doing."

"As you can see, I'm just fine." I walked him to the door, wanting to get this mortifying scene over with. Twice

I had embarrassed myself with a kiss. Next time, I'd have to let him lead. "See you when I see you, then."

He nodded and a serious look came over his face, pushing my playful thoughts away. "This can't happen again, Harmony. I'm serious this time."

I nodded back, feeling cold inside. He clearly didn't feel the same way I did. I stood a little straighter. "No worries there." I would not make the mistake of making the first move ever again.

So much for next time.

Chapter Sixteen

"Thanks, Tiff. This is great. I didn't think you'd be up for hosting this week." I sipped my beer and dug into an assortment of pub food. I loved the open concept floorplan of their ranch, and it was nice being on the outskirts of town.

No prying eyes.

"I didn't host." Tiffany laughed. "Matt did all the work. It's the perks of having a pub owner as a fiancé. And no, I didn't clean the house, either. He did. I was going to hire a housekeeper with my inheritance from Grammy, but Matt actually likes cleaning. Can you believe that?"

"I can." Zoe winked. She had always been an organized neat queen, who had to be in control, but Chaz had really gotten her to loosen up.

"He's a keeper," I said, remembering the look on Byron's face when he walked out the door. I still couldn't get rid of the hollow feeling which had crept into my entire being the moment he was gone. My universe wouldn't forsake me at a time like this. But it had and even with the love of my best friends, I felt lost. "You're lucky." Then I pinched the bridge of my nose in an attempt to keep my emotions at bay. I faked a sniffle as a cover up when I caught Zoe's calculating stare. "Damn allergies."

"I might have something in my purse." She was such a mom.

"Thanks, babe, I already took something. It just hasn't kicked in yet." I sniffed again for good measure, and my care-giving bestie settled in beside Morti.

"And he knows how hard it is to take care of twins," Morti added as she scooched over. "He's back at work and you have such great employees, you don't have to go in unless you want to. Plus, you have your mother and sister as a big help, which is awesome. I'm so happy for you, Tiff. I wish I had all that." She sipped her diet cola, nibbling on a loaded potato skin.

"It will happen, Morti. I can feel it. Just keep the faith." Zoe smiled and took a drink of her chardonnay.

"Speaking of happening...what happened when you talked to Zander?" Tiff sipped her Martini.

"Well, he did *not* reduce my sentence, but I do believe I put him in a difficult situation to begin with. He had to respond to the town's complaint, and even I can admit I have a few issues I need help with. SAA was just a cover."

"You believe him?" Morti asked.

"If he was lying, he's one hell of an actor. He claims he only suggested Byron because he knew he was the best. From personal experience, no less. I guess Byron helped him out years ago, but he didn't say how, so I'm assuming it was personal. The SAA part was for show for the town, and probably a little bit for himself."

"Did he tell you why Byron feels he still owes him a favor?" Tiff asked. "I mean, if Zander did something for Byron and then Byron later helped him out, it would seem to me that they are even."

"One would think, but Byron wouldn't tell me any more than Zander would." They were both so frustrating. Not telling me made my mind wander through all sorts of crazy scenarios, which were probably far worse than the truth.

"It's nice that Byron's back." Zoe finished her wine. "He was gone longer than I thought he would be, and I have to admit, I was a little worried he wasn't coming back."

"You and me both. And I used to think his coming back would be more than nice." I pushed my plate away, no longer hungry. "Not so much now."

"Trouble in paradise?" Morti quirked a brow. Morti and I had always given each other a hard time, but in a loving best friend kind of way. Deep down we knew we were all there for each other, no matter what.

"That's the problem. There's not supposed to *be* a paradise." I blew out my breath, regretting ever crossing the line.

"Awe, what happened, doll?" Tiff rubbed my arm.

"So, you all know I kissed him in the pub in front of Zander a while back, right?"

They nodded.

"That had been the start of my recklessness. Just to teach Zander a lesson, when all that happened was me discovering that Byron is more than a pretty face."

We had chemistry.

"Yes, but that was just for show and to prove a point." Morti nodded. "I remember the look on Zander's face. I'd say he got the message."

"Well, so did Byron. I kissed him again last night, in my apartment, with no one around and no lesson to teach." I looked at each of them and bit my bottom lip on a groan. "And he kissed me back."

"Oh, my God, yay!" Zoe clapped her hands. She was such the romantic. "So, what's the problem?"

"He regretted it immediately." A lump formed in my throat over that admission. It still hurt like hell.

The girls all gasped.

"Did he say that exactly?" Tiff asked.

"Well, no, but you should have seen his face. And then he said, and I quote, 'This can never happen again. I mean it this time, Harmony.'" My face fell. Repeating his words caused the hollow feeling inside me to get bigger. "I was so embarrassed. Just when I think I have a good read on him, I find out I don't. I didn't mean to kiss him, it just happened after he told me I was beautiful just the way I am. Do you know how long I've waited for a man to say that to me?" I covered my face with my hands, feeling my cheeks blaze with heat. "Maybe I do need help for a sex addiction after all."

"No, he needs help for not expressing himself better." Morti grabbed my hand and made me look at her. "He's definitely confusing you with his hot and cold behavior, and I don't like it one bit."

"Well, he does have some sort of oath like Chaz, I suppose," Zoe mused, "but I do agree he could be better at explaining his actions. I mean, he *did* kiss you back, and that's on him." She winced. "I'm, sorry, Harm."

"It's okay. I'm over it. It's just frustrating, is all, especially because he's not really my therapist. I'm not paying him. And as for being my sponsor, he's not even really that. He's just helping an old friend out. I'll be glad when this program is over and he can leave, because clearly, he doesn't want to be with me after the dust settles, so to speak." I brushed away a random tear, feeling like a fool for getting vulnerable with him in the first place. "I think he's never met someone like me. I'm just entertainment for him, is all."

"Well, two can play at that game." Tiff handed me a tissue box. "You can't hide passion like that. We've all seen the way he looks at you when he knows you're not watching. He cares about you, too. I say call him on his bluff. You can't kiss him if you don't see him. Absence makes the heart grow fonder, and all that."

"That's true. If he doesn't care about you, then he won't miss seeing you." Zoe looked pensive. "So far you're still winning the bet by not having sex with Byron, but I'm betting he won't be able to stay away from you much longer."

"I think you're all crazy, but hey, avoiding him sounds good to me right now." My heart couldn't take much more from Mr. Byron Storm.

At least the rumors weren't affecting my business anymore. And the rumors weren't pushing men away anymore, either. I guess it didn't really matter who the rumor spreader was because I wasn't interested in dating anyone anytime soon.

Maybe things were finally turning a corner for the better.

"Oн, my goddess, things can't get any worse." My heart sank to my feet one week later as I stood in my store.

I stared at the extensive damage to my shop and wondered how it would ever be the same again. I'd been avoiding Byron, and we had entered the first week of May. A whole new month with new possibilities. Bye Bye April and all the fools from that month. Clearly the rumors weren't working, so someone had upped their game.

They'd trashed my shop!

"This is why I kept harping on you to get your security camera fixed, Harm." Officer Pickles stood there, shaking his head with his hands on his hips. "We'll dust for prints, but I doubt the perp was careless enough to leave any evidence behind."

"Thanks, Don." Byron was supposed to fix that for me, but I had been avoiding him, nixing that idea. "Hal said he would fix it for me." My brother owned Hal's Hardware and was pretty handy.

"Better late than never, just get it done so I don't have to come back to another scene like this." Pickles tipped his hat then headed over to join his CSI team.

We had gone to high school together. His parents had thought it was adorable to name him Dillard Donald Pickles aka Dill Pickles. Our classmates had had a field day, but Dill who went by Don these days, had the last laugh when he'd become a police officer and had arrested or written tickets for each and every one of his bullies over the years.

My insurance adjuster was coming later, after the CSI team was finished. I looked around at the mess. Nothing was stolen, but every display case was smashed. The front window was broken. The lights were crushed. My oils covered the floor with broken glass. And extra attention was directed at anything to do with witchcraft.

This latest action went way beyond mere rumors...

Clearly this person despised me.

What if they wanted to hurt me physically? Or maybe wanted me dead? I would never admit to anyone that I was a little scared. I hunted with my brothers, but I didn't have a pistol permit. I didn't have any weapons in my shop, other than the infamous broomstick.

Maybe I needed to change that.

I headed to the back of my store and examined the

remaining books that hadn't been touched. Well, there was that at least.

"Why didn't you call me?" came a voice from behind that sent electricity through my body like it always did. *Sponsors are just a phone call away, so use them,* was the motto of our SAA program group host, Dr. Shirley.

I steeled my reserve and slowly turned around, raising my chin a notch. "Because this matter doesn't concern you, Mr. Storm." I crossed my arms. "There's no chance of me attacking any men here, so I don't need a sponsor for this."

He narrowed his eyes. "Harmony, don't you think we're past—"

"It's Ms. Jones to you." I shrugged. "Just keeping things professional."

He sighed and ran a hand through his long hair, looking hotter than a man had a right to. "That's not what I meant."

I tore my gaze away. "Well, it's what I mean."

"Fine. I give up. You win. Care to tell me what happened here, Ms. Jones?" He looked tired, like he hadn't slept in a week.

It would feel good to think maybe I had caused that when I ghosted him because that would mean that he cared, but I had learned my lesson the hard way. His insomnia had nothing to do with me.

"I would think it's obvious." I swept my arm wide. "Someone vandalized my shop, but I don't know who because my security cameras are still broken."

His voice softened, and his eyes gentled. "I would have gladly fixed them, but you never called."

I looked away. "And I won't. I no longer need your services. My brother, Hal, is going to fix them."

"Fine. I guess you don't need my help for anything then." I looked up in time to see him shove his hands in his jeans pockets, his face clearly frustrated, and he didn't even try to school his features this time.

"Nope, I don't need you." *Want you, yes, but I refuse to need you.* I kept inspecting what inventory I had left that wasn't ruined, afraid to look at him too long in fear of caving and begging him to like me, to...stay.

"Harm...Ms. Jones, I'm just trying to be here for you if you'll let me. I'm trying to keep my promise to—"

"Whatever is between you and Zander is between the two of you. I'm just fine on my own."

"Dammit Harmony, I am trying to keep my promise to you, not him." His voice was sharper than I had ever heard it.

That gave me pause, and my hand stilled, but I didn't say anything.

"I told you I would be here for you, and I meant it."

"Fine. If I feel the urge to *kiss* anyone again, I'll call. No need to see me in person. You know, for safety's sake. I wouldn't want to risk putting you in harm's way. Part of the twelve steps, and all." My gaze met his, and this time, I didn't look away.

His eyes grew sad, and I almost yielded under his spell

when he said, "You're not going to let this matter drop, are you?"

"And why would she do that? You're supposed to be helping her." Zander joined us at the back of the shop. Placing his hands on his hips, he cast a curious glance back and forth between the two of us and raised a dark eyebrow. "What matter?"

And just like that, the spell was broken.

"The matter of me trying to investigate who might be after me." I stood tall. "He's worried about my safety...and his own." That much was true but for far different reasons than the Honorable Judge Jackson could fathom.

"That's Byron for you. Always trying to be the hero and take care of everyone to a fault, even if it gets him in trouble." Zander gave Byron a serious look.

"You should talk." Byron stared right back.

An unspoken conversation passed between them. While I was dying to know the truth of their relationship, I just wanted everything over so my life could return to normal. Heartache sucked.

Zander broke eye contact first. "That's why I'm here now. To do my job and see that justice is served and keep you both from getting into trouble."

Did this have to do with me, or the secret they were keeping?

"No worries, boys, I can take care of myself. No one is going to get into trouble, especially over me." I walked towards the front of my shop. "Now if you'll excuse me, my insurance adjuster is here, and you two are in the way." I opened the door and gestured for them both to leave.

"We're not done with this conversation," Byron said for my ears only, sending chills down my spine in a good but dangerous way as he walked by me.

I cleared my throat...twice. "Like I said, I'll call if I need help."

"Clearly I misjudged your ability to take care of yourself, Ms. Jones." Zander gave me a head nod as he walked by. "I think you'll be just fine on your own."

"That's what I've been trying to tell everyone." I let the insurance adjuster in and closed the door firmly behind her but couldn't resist sneaking a peek out the window as the men walked away. At the last second, Byron's eyes met mine.

Well, hell.

Chapter Seventeen

It was the second week of May. A lot of progress had been made on repairing my shop, but no progress had been made on catching the vandal. No progress had been made on getting Byron to miss me, either.

Stubborn man.

I kept ignoring him like Tiffany had suggested, but my absence didn't appear to make his heart grow fonder. He'd said our conversation wasn't over, but that was a week ago, and I hadn't seen or heard from him since. Granted, I'd basically told him, *Don't call me, I'll call you*, but I had expected him to at least make an effort. I had to face the harsh reality...

Maybe I had read him wrong, and he just really wasn't that into me.

"You're all set, Harm." My brother, Hal, walked outside to join me as I sat on the bench by the curb.

Lighthouse Lane was hopping in the spring with the

temperatures rising and May flowers blooming. I tried to spend as much time as I could outside, knowing what the winter would bring. Plus, it was still depressing knowing it was going to be a while before I would be ready to fully reopen.

I shielded my eyes from the sun and peeked over at him. "Wow, that was quick. Both the front and back cameras are working again?"

"They sure are. I added more secure locks on both doors as well."

"Thanks, bro." I nudged him with my shoulder.

"Any time, bean." He echoed my father's nickname for me.

"What's going on over at *Walt's Single Malts?*" I looked across the street at the liquor store parking lot. They had a tent outside with a bunch of tables set up, a food truck, a cigar bar, and live music. "Is that Dad?"

"Yup, and I'm headed there myself. The rest of the boys will be there after they get off work."

"Why?"

"Walt and Al are hosting a checkers competition, with prizes to both the liquor store and *Shanker's Smoke Shop.* It kind of stinks that the cigar shop is on the outskirts of town, but he has quite the collection to choose from out there. I hope I win one of the prizes." Hal rubbed his hands together and winked at me. "See ya, sis."

I waved as he jogged across the street. My jaw fell open when I saw my mother and Peter's mother playing hostess in their bedazzled checkered shirts and skirts.

Chaz, Matt, and Finn were there, along with the barbers and lumberjacks and... I sucked in a sharp breath...

Zander and Byron.

As if he had eyes in the back of his head, he turned around and caught me staring at him. He said something to Zander and then started walking my way. I looked left then right, anywhere but at him, as I tried to find a way to disappear.

"Hi, Harmony." He stood before me in his trademark jeans and eighties rock band t-shirt, with his hair pulled back in a low ponytail. He didn't smile, just stared at me with those kind, compassionate, honey brown eyes.

"Hi, Byron." I looked away before I got sucked in.

"May I?" He gestured to the bench.

I shrugged. "Sure. It's not my bench." It was by the streetlamp in front of my store.

He sat, and an uncomfortable silence hovered between us.

He spoke first. "I see your security cameras are fixed."

"Hal finished them just a little while ago." Our hands nearly touched on the bench, so I folded mine in my lap.

He glanced over his shoulder and looked into my storefront window. "How are the repairs to your store coming?"

"Good. They're almost done." I hated how awkward things were between us. I could tell he wanted to say more, and I wasn't sure why he didn't. We hadn't talked in a week, and all he wanted to talk about was small talk.

"Can I ask how you're doing in the program?"

"Almost done with that as well."

"Good." He finally looked at me. "I'm here if you need me, you know."

"I know." He'd made it clear he was here for me as a sponsor and nothing more. "You were loud and clear."

"Do you want to talk about anything?"

"No." I had my walls back up, and he was the one who had put them there. What did he expect from me?

"Okay. If you change your mind—"

"I'll call. Got it." I looked away from him back over to the liquor store, trying to focus on anything else so I wouldn't cry.

Zander waved to get Byron's attention then motioned him over, pointing at the checkerboard.

"Guess I have to go. I think it's our turn."

"Guess so."

He stood. "You know we never did finish our conversation."

Now he wanted to talk? He'd wasted all that time, and all week for that matter. "I really have nothing more to say that's not professional, so it's probably best we don't talk about anything personal."

"Well, maybe I *do* have something to say. Harmony, I—"

"Byron!" Zander shouted. "Come on, man. We're up."

"You'd better go." I stared up at him. "You don't want to lose your turn and owe Zander another favor." A lump formed in my throat, and I blinked back tears, refusing to let them fall. I couldn't go back to normal and pretend like everything was fine knowing he didn't feel the same way as I felt about him.

A muscle in his jaw flexed, then he turned around and left without another word.

~

"THIS ISN'T WORKING," I said as I stood at the counter of *Tiffany's Titillating Touch* a few days later.

"You can take your break now, Trixy." Tiffany smiled at her receptionist who wore her bleach blonde hair in pigtails.

"Call if you need me." Trixy waved and then headed toward the small break room in the back.

The waiting room was dead at the moment, with clients getting massages with Maxim and Lucy in their respective rooms. Or at least that's what Tiffany had told me when I sent her a text and asked if I could stop by to talk.

"What isn't working, doll?" Motherhood had really given her a lot more patience, because I was even annoying myself with my whining, but I couldn't help it. She handed me cucumber water.

"Thanks." I took a big sip. "I tried ignoring Byron like you said, hoping he would realize he did actually care about me, but he didn't call or stop by for an entire week. Absence made my heart grow fonder, but I don't think it did a thing for his."

"I thought you two talked during the checkers tournament at *Walt's Single Malts?* Matt said Byron was Zander's partner and they almost had to forfeit their turn because Byron was in front of your shop talking to you."

"He only came to talk to me when he saw me staring at him. And then he wasted time on small talk, until it was too late to talk about anything important before he got called back to the game. He has to be the most frustrating man I've ever met."

"How did he leave it? Did he say anything else?"

"Well, he did say we still hadn't finished our conversation from the day my shop got vandalized."

"What do you think he wants to talk about?"

"I don't know if he wants to talk about me not calling him when I was in danger or if he wants to talk about my embarrassing kiss and him telling me that couldn't happen again. Neither one is his responsibility. I only need to call him if I'm in sexual danger, not physical, and there is no chance of that happening, so we don't need to talk."

"Well, you two are friends now, so it's natural he worries."

"I'm sure he just wants to finish his favor for Zander, and I genuinely do believe he wants to help me, but that's all, so there really isn't anything more to talk about. He wanted to keep things professional, so that's what I'm doing." I rested my chin on my palm, feeling mentally exhausted and physically drained.

"Then why are you complaining if you're doing what you want?" Tiffany was only asking questions I had been asking myself.

I sighed. "Because it's not what I want. It's what *he* wants."

"So, what do *you* want then?"

"I want him to feel the same way about me because he wants to, not because I want him to. I can't go back to just being his friend after I know what it's like to kiss him."

"I thought you said he kissed you back." She sipped her lemon water.

"He did, but I know he only kissed me back because he's human, but that doesn't mean he wants anything more from me."

"You don't know that for sure. Just be patient. Maybe he was respecting your wishes and giving you space. You might be overthinking this."

"Maybe. I know he's trying to be ethical. I get that but not once did he indicate he wanted something with me later on." I shook my head. "I don't know what to do anymore. What to say. I never expected to feel this way." I swallowed a sob before it could break free. "It's killing me, and I can't even tell him."

"Why not? You have nothing to lose."

I gaped at her, coming to my emotional senses. "Are you crazy? He would leave town for sure then."

"And then you would have your answer." She shrugged as if it were that simple. "You said avoiding him wasn't working, so maybe telling him how you feel will. Either way, you'll get the clarity you're searching for."

"I don't know, maybe." Maybe it would work. Maybe it wouldn't. Maybe this was the dumbest idea I'd ever had...

Maybe I was insane.

Maybe I needed to cross that line.

Later that night, I parked my car at Quincy Cottage, carried a picnic basket, and knocked on the front door.

Byron opened the door, wearing a pair of joggers, no shirt, and surprised sleepy eyes. "Harmony?" He ran a hand over his messy hair.

I struggled to pull my gaze away from his naked glorious chest. "I brought a peace offering. Did I come at a bad time?" I swallowed hard. The struggle was real.

"No, no." He held the door open. "Come in. I fell asleep on the couch while I was reading."

"Anything good?" I walked past him and carried my basket into the kitchen, if only to change the distracting view.

"It's a mystery about a woman who's really hard to figure out." He followed me to the kitchen, snagging a t-shirt from the couch along the way and pulling it on. I wasn't sure if I was happy or sad about that.

"Sounds interesting." I pulled out cartons of Chinese food and set them on the table to keep my hands busy.

"It keeps me on my toes, I'll say that." He grabbed a couple of beers from the refrigerator and popped the tops, then handed me one.

"Thanks. I hope you're hungry." I sat down and took

the plate he handed me then dished up some Sweet and Sour Chicken, Fried Rice, and Egg Rolls.

"I'm starved." He dished up Beef with Broccoli, Chow Mein noodles, and Wonton Soup, then we both took a moment to eat.

I cracked open a fortune cookie and pulled out the tiny white piece of paper. "You are in charge of your own happiness." Yes, I was, but I had promised myself I would never make the first move again.

Crashing and burning wasn't fun.

He picked up a fortune cookie and broke it open as well. Pulling out the paper, he read, "There's a fork in the road. Choose wisely." He quirked a brow at me.

"Good advice." I nibbled on my cookie.

His gaze dropped to my lips, then snapped back to my eyes. "Don't get me wrong, I'm glad you're here. But can I ask what this peace offering is about?"

I inhaled a deep breath and let it out slowly. "You said you wanted to finish our conversation, so I'm here to finish it."

"Okay, then. Let's get comfortable. This might take a while." He stood and grabbed us two more beers then carried them over to the couch.

I joined him. "I realize I've been a little distant. Maybe even a little harsh. I'm sorry for doing that. It wasn't really fair of me."

"You don't have to apologize. You're entitled to your feelings." His voice rang with sincerity and regret.

"And you're entitled to yours." I shook my head, still feeling the embarrassment of practically jumping his bones. "I shouldn't have forced myself on you. No one deserves that. Good grief, maybe I am as bad as everyone says."

"Harmony, you didn't force anything on me. I'll admit you took me by surprise for a moment, but I didn't have to respond. That's on me."

"I get it. You're human, so you reacted, but for me it's more than that." I couldn't look at him when I added, "I care about you a lot."

He lifted my chin until my gaze met his. "I care about you, too." He blew out a frustrated breath. "This isn't as cut and dry as you'd like it to be. We've spent a lot of time together. It's only natural we've grown close. I worry about you, and I want to be in your life still. I want to be there for you when you need someone and to help you."

Ugh. He was listening, but he wasn't hearing me. "I don't think you understand what I'm trying to say."

His brow puckered. "Maybe not. What are you saying? That you don't want me around anymore?"

"No, yes, I don't know." I downed my beer. "I'm not very good at this." I felt my pulse quicken. What if I couldn't do this? Why had I let Tiffany talk me into opening myself up to vulnerability?

"It's okay. Take your time and just tell me how you feel." He spoke in his usual calming therapeutic voice.

I sat with a death grip on the bottle while I took a few deep breaths. Peeling back the edge of the label was easier than making eye contact as I worked up the courage to divulge my true feelings.

"Harm?"

"Fine." My voice boomed through the silence of the cottage. It was now or never. There would be no turning back after this. "You want to know how I feel? I'm falling for you, okay? Like really falling for you."

He blinked. "Harmony—"

"Just let me get this out." The damage was already done, I might as well go full-in. "I've never felt this way about anyone, and it has nothing to do with a stupid sex addiction. You get me like no one else ever has. So, yes, I want you in my life, but not as my sponsor or therapist. I want you as my boyfriend."

He squeezed his eyes shut for a moment then looked at me with...pity. "Harmony, you know I can't. I—"

"I get it." I surged to my feet. I couldn't be near him. If I stayed a moment longer, I was going to lose it in front of him. He'd taken my heart, and I refused to let him take my dignity. "This was a stupid idea. I never should have told you my real feelings. You don't feel the same way about me. That has become inherently clear. Now every time you're with me, you're going to pity me, and I can't take that." I headed for the kitchen counter.

"Harmony, wait. Where are you going?"

"Home. I-I just need to be away from you." I grabbed my basket and turned toward the front door. "Session officially over, Doc."

"But we're not finished talking. You're crying. Don't leave like this." I could hear him moving behind me.

"It's okay. I know you don't want me." I reached my hand for the doorknob and started to pull it open. "I'll be fine."

His hand pushed the door firmly closed, and I could feel his breath on the back of my neck. "Dammit, Harmony, it's not okay, and it's not about what I want. It's about what I can't have but am helpless to resist." He spun me around and his mouth swooped down over mine with such passion and need, my head spun. The next thing I knew I was in his arms as he carried me to his bedroom.

What that meant, I had no clue, but for once in my life, I was done overthinking.

Chapter Eighteen

yron's lips never broke contact with mine as he laid me down on the king size bed in the master bedroom of *Quincy Cottage*. His hands were everywhere as he knelt over me. I couldn't think straight as I reached up and plunged my hands through his glorious hair, free from its usual ponytail and bit his bottom lip.

With a low growl, he broke contact long enough to sweep off my t-shirt and bra, adding his t-shirt to the pile on the floor. He took a moment to worship my breasts from the moonlight reflecting off Freedom Lake, streaming through the window.

My breasts were small, but I'd never been self-conscious. I was happy with my tomboy-like body, never really caring what other people thought. For the first time, I wanted so badly for Byron to approve. I hated feeling vulnerable, but the look in his eyes told me everything I needed to know.

"You're so beautiful," he whispered, seconds before lowering his head and taking my nipple into his mouth.

I arched my back, squirming and moaning beneath him. He chuckled deep in his throat and then gave the other nipple equal attention. I ran my short fingernails over his shoulders and down his back as far as I could reach.

He kissed his way down my stomach, lingering on my belly button. Undoing my jeans, he tugged them down over my hips and looked up at me in surprise.

"I-I don't like underwear," I barely breathed.

"I'm glad." His voice sounded husky.

"B-Byron please."

"Shhh, babe." He gently spread my thighs apart and nestled himself between my legs, kissing me everywhere except where I throbbed the most.

"Byron, damn you." I gripped his shoulders, digging my nails in.

He grunted, then parted my folds and stroked me intimately, slipping one finger inside. Biting my thigh, he added a second finger and ground his thumb into my sweet spot, circling hard until I screamed.

Only then did he dive his tongue deep.

I saw stars.

My body convulsed over and over to the rhythm of his thrusts. When I could no longer move and lie there spent from sweet exhaustion, he joined me fully naked on the bed, having removed his joggers at some point. A pack of condoms appeared from out of nowhere, but two could play this game.

"My turn," I whispered as I rolled him over and lay on top of him.

"Wait, it's been a while. I might not—"

"Shhh," I mimicked and started kissing my way down his chest, flicking both nipples with my tongue then lingering on his belly button like he had mine.

"Jesus, Harm." He moaned.

I grinned, slowly sliding my naked body further down his. My eyes grew wide over the size of him. "You're beautiful," I said with a breathy voice, and meant it.

Running my hand up and down the length of him, squeezing tight, he grew harder, which I hadn't thought possible. His hands swept through my short hair, gripping and pulling lightly. I ran my tongue around the tip of his penis and squeezed his testicles ever so slightly, then took the length of him deep inside my mouth as far as it could go and sucked hard. Using my tongue and hands together, I brought him to the brink of release.

Before I knew what was happening, he pulled me up his body, donned a condom, and thrust himself into my vagina.

I cried out.

He stilled. "Oh, God, did I hurt you?"

"No, but I might you." I ground myself down hard on top of him until he was fully sheathed.

"Harmony," my name came out on a half-moan, half-whisper of need.

That was all I needed to hear.

I started riding him for all I was worth.

He ran his hands over my hair and face then gently wrapped them around my neck, stroking my vocal cords with his thumbs. Spreading his palms wide, he ran them down my chest, cupping my breasts, then slid them down to grip my hips. He squeezed his eyes shut as he urged me on faster, a muscle in his jaw pulsing.

I slid my hand behind me and squeezed his scrotum. That did it. He flipped me over, pounding into me, and I welcomed every thrust. Whipping my head back and forth, I shouted his name as a massive wave of pleasure swept over me, my body trembling with aftershocks. Seconds later, he cried out as he stiffened, his whole body shaking before he collapsed on top of me.

He started to roll off, but I wrapped my legs and arms around him.

"Don't move."

He buried his face in the crook of my neck as an answer and relaxed his body against me, as he stroked my arm.

I don't know how long we stayed like that, but our bodies had cooled, and our heartbeats had slowed. We both dozed off for a while. When he rolled off me this time, I let him go. My body chilled instantly, so I grabbed my clothes and got dressed.

There was a difference in the air suddenly.

When I stood and turned around, he was fully dressed as well and looking at me with an expression I couldn't read. "It's getting late."

"Yeah, I should probably get going. Don't want people to see my Love Bug here all night." I joked.

He didn't smile. "Probably not a good idea."

I frowned. "You're talking about the car, right?"

He hesitated a moment, but I noticed, before responding, "Of course."

An awkward silence fell between us.

"Well, then, I'll just get my basket and be on my way." I headed for the door where I'd dropped my picnic basket after he'd stopped me from leaving.

He followed me but did nothing to stop me this time.

I turned around and stared at him. "What's wrong?"

Something flashed in his eyes. "Nothing."

"I can tell something is wrong. Talk to me." I pleaded with my eyes, hating that I felt weak, like I was on the verge of losing my soul.

"I..." His shoulders slumped on a sigh. "I'm fine."

Pain sliced through me. "You regret making love to me, don't you?" I managed to get out past the lump in my throat. What had we done, and how was I ever going to recover from this?

He looked up at the ceiling and ran a hand through his hair. "I told you it's not about what I want. It shouldn't have happened."

"Dammit, Byron, this time you're the one who made the first move," I raised my voice, unable to remain in control.

"Because you tempt me, woman! I can't resist you no

matter how hard I try. That doesn't make it right." He raised his voice right back.

"You should have let me go." My voice trembled, making me more upset. "I knew you didn't want me."

"You call *that* not wanting you?" He thrust his finger towards the bedroom. "Dammit, Harmony, what more do I have to do?"

"Love me, but you don't!" My tears started to fall. I'd said it. That should be enough.

He stared at me at a loss for words.

"I'm an enigma for you, Byron Storm. A pretty plaything. You might want me physically, but that's not enough for me." I squelched the hollow feeling that had returned with a vengeance. I wasn't about to let it swallow me whole.

"I keep telling you it doesn't matter what I want. I have a moral responsibility as your sponsor—"

"Don't give me that crap. Just face it, Byron. You don't love me like I love you, and I can't be your friend anymore."

"Harmony, wait." He reached out to me.

"I'm done waiting." Tears streamed down my face as I turned around and ran out the door.

ONE WEEK LATER, I sat in my apartment for girls' night, feeling completely numb.

"How are you, Harm?" Tiffany shoulder hugged me as she walked through the door, carrying a case of beer.

"Not good." I sat on a barstool in my pajamas.

"Aww don't you worry, hon. We're here for you." Zoe gave me a hug as well and then carried a big pan of lasagna to my kitchen counter. She liked to cook and feed people when they were down.

"Who needs a man, anyway." Morti carried in a loaf of bread, a carton of ice cream, and a box of tissues.

"I do." I blew my nose. "And I *hate* that I do."

"Have you heard from him?" Tiffany popped open a beer and set it in front of me, then passed around Champagne for her, chardonnay for Zoe, and a diet cola for Morti.

"Not in a week. Memorial Weekend is next week, and he was supposed to be my plus one to all the events. We agreed on that months ago. So much for still wanting to be in my life." I felt like the biggest fool, yet I missed him horribly.

"But I thought you said you didn't want to be his friend anymore," Zoe said gently, dishing up food for me and passing more around for everyone else.

"I did and I don't. I just didn't expect it to hurt this much. The thought of never seeing his face or talking to him or touching him ever again is too much to bear."

"I know it's hard, doll, but you don't want to be with someone if they only want you physically, do you?"

"I honestly don't know. I know my worth, but damn this

is hard. I never expected that conversation to be the end of whatever we were. He made the first move this time, but he's right. I pressed him for more which pushed him to do something he now regrets. I feel like it's all my fault. He can't help it if he doesn't love me back. And now he has to live with unnecessary guilt even though this whole sentence has been a farce. I should have just stuck to my gut and gone to jail. I'd be out by now with my heart still intact."

"Are you sure he doesn't love you?" Zoe kept shaking her head over and over. "We all saw how he looked at you. I'm telling you there was more than chemistry between you two. We couldn't all be so wrong."

"I agree. Something doesn't seem right. Did he actually say the words?" Tiffany refilled our drinks.

I thought about that. "I guess he never said that he didn't love me, but he didn't say that he did, either. He said, '*It's not about what I want. It shouldn't have happened.*' That's a far cry from telling me he loved me back."

"Maybe he does love you, but he can't pursue anything with you until after your sentence is finished." Morti sipped her soda.

"Then he would have said that, but he didn't."

"Yes, but you do have a tendency to run away when conversations get uncomfortable," Zoe said.

"I do not." *Did I?*

"Sorry, doll, but as your best friends, we keep it real. You've done it with us before when you've gotten frustrated."

"I have?" I blinked, completely unaware of this trait.

"You especially do it with your mother." Morti nodded. "I get it. My father drives me crazy sometimes."

"Am I really that bad?" I blew my nose.

"You're not bad, hon." Zoe squeezed my hand. "It's just something you might want to work on. You can't always leave just because you're not hearing what you want to hear. If you stick around, you might see things aren't always as bad as they seem."

"Maybe I actually do need therapy."

"I love therapy." Tiff nodded. "Mine even schedules my sessions online, which is so convenient with the twins."

"I agree." Zoe fished a card out of her purse and handed it to me. "Here's mine. You would love her. We talk once a week."

"But I have you guys."

"And we are always here for you to vent to, but it's so important to have someone who's impartial and can offer objective opinions and sound advice," Zoe added.

"I can't say much on the matter." Morti shrugged. "I get my therapy by reading books on self-help, but hey, it's worth a shot."

I took the card. "Thanks, babes. I really do appreciate each of you so much."

"What are you going to do?" Tiff asked.

"I don't know."

"Maybe call him," Zoe offered.

"And say what?"

"Ask him directly if he loves you?" Morti said.

"Fine, but I'm doing it right now with you all here in case I need you."

"We're not going anywhere." Tiffany handed me my phone.

I dialed Byron's number. It rang four times, and I almost hung up, but then someone answered it.

"Hello?" said a woman's voice.

I sucked in a sharp breath.

"Is anyone there?" she asked again.

"Wrong number," I said then promptly hung up.

"Wrong number?" Tiffany gaped at me.

"What's going on?" Morti arched a brow.

"Who was that?" Zoe blurted.

My head was spinning as I stared at all of them and said, "Some woman just answered Byron's phone. He doesn't love me because, clearly, he's in love with someone else."

Chapter Nineteen

"I can't believe he left. Just up and left without even saying goodbye." I sipped a cup of steaming hot tea at my mother's house the next day. After crying myself to sleep, I couldn't take it anymore. We might not always get along, but she was my mother.

"And a woman answered the phone you say?" My mother set her teacup back on its saucer as she studied me.

"Yup."

"Yes, darling."

I blinked. "Excuse me?"

"It's not *yup*. It's yes." She sat up straighter. "People will think you're uneducated if you talk like a simpleton."

I just stared at her. Really stared. "I can't believe you're talking about manners at a time like this."

She blinked at me. "I'm just trying to help, dear. Men don't like—"

"I don't care what men like, Mother." I set my tea

down more forcefully than I meant to. "Quit trying to change me."

"Why, whatever do you mean? I'm not trying to change you. I'm just trying to polish you."

"Well, I don't need polishing. Why can't you just love me the way that I am? I have never been good enough for you."

She gaped at me, her eyes filling with tears. "Is that what you think?"

I let out a long sigh, feeling a lifetime of exhaustion playing this game. "I'm sorry if I'm hurting your feelings, Mom, but this talk is long overdue."

"I had no idea you felt that way." She sniffled, dabbing her eyes with a tissue. "I know you've made comments before, but I didn't think you were serious. Have you always felt this way?"

"Pretty much."

She let out a little whimper. "I don't know what to say."

"I know that you love me, and I love you, too. I just feel like you're not happy with me as your only daughter."

"Oh, honey, that couldn't be further from the truth." She shook her head sadly. "You're so beautiful and independent. I admire how courageous and brave you are. I never would have had the gumption to start my own business. You get that from your father. You're so smart." She lifted her chin a notch. "You get that from me. I might not always understand your choices, but I couldn't be prouder of you."

It seemed as if I'd misunderstood her as well. "Then why have you always tried to change me?"

"You seemed so lonely. I really was just trying to help you find a man. All I know is the way that I am, so I didn't know any other way to give you advice. I never meant for you to think that I was disappointed or unhappy with you."

I kicked myself for all the time we had wasted by worrying about upsetting the other person. "From here on out, how about we tell each other how we feel. I hear that's a thing." I chuckled softly, then covered my basis by adding, "And we only offer advice when solicited. Agreed?"

"Agreed." She hugged me. "As for that man, it's his loss if he can't see what an amazing woman you are."

"Thanks, Mom."

"It's not your fault that he left, you know. Do you have any idea why?" She looked genuinely perplexed. "I'm no expert, but he sure seemed smitten with you. Everyone said so."

"I don't know. Maybe the woman who answered his phone is someone he's interested in. I think I pushed him into something he wasn't ready for, and I compromised his ethics. I don't know if he can get over that. Why else would he have left?"

"Well, dear, maybe it's time you stop looking for a man and just focus on you. When you least expect it is when life usually sends its blessings." She patted my hand. "I'm so proud of you. You're nearly finished with this program, and your business is almost fully repaired.

You're a fighter. You didn't let that silly rumor spreader ruin you."

"I just hope it's the last I have to deal with that."

"I can't imagine anyone that desperate to keep things going. I'm sure you can rest easy now."

"I sure hope so because I can't take any more. I might be strong, but even I have my breaking point."

IT WAS the last week of May. Memorial Weekend.

I was in mourning over Byron, because I didn't think I would ever see him again, but I was picking up the pieces and moving on. It was hard because five months of knowing him had been long enough for me to fall head-over-heels in love with him.

I didn't regret it.

He'd taught me many things about myself, and I wouldn't have turned a corner with my mother if it hadn't been for his encouragement. I decided to take my mother's advice and go solo since he wasn't around to be my plus one.

I passed by Heather and...Peter Sherman!

My mouth fell open.

She gave me a little wave, and I waved back with a wide smile, genuinely happy for them. She must have taken my advice and gone after what she wanted. I was glad it had worked out for her. They sat at a table in the park in front of the gazebo with Tabatha, listening to Finn entertain the crowd. My heart warmed for them as well. I spotted Zoe, Chaz, Tiffany, Matt, and Morticia at a nearby table.

Turning in that direction, Phoenix gave me a two-finger salute. She had reached out to me after my shop was vandalized. Differences aside, she wanted me to know that no one deserved to have that happen to them, and she offered to help with whatever I needed. I respected and appreciated that.

I gave her a head nod and kept walking.

Rose Theodore stuck her nose in the air and turned her back to me, talking with a group of people in front of her display on the history of Mayflower. My lips tipped up a little as I shook my head. Rose would never change, and that was okay.

I had almost reached my friends' table when Zander stepped into my path.

"Can I have a word with you, Ms. Jones?"

I blinked. *What now?* "Am I in trouble?"

"Not today." He guided me to a table further away, and we sat down. "I have good news for you."

I crossed my arms over my midsection. "No offense, but coming from you, I'm a bit skeptical."

"Fair enough, but this news I think you'll like."

"I'm all ears."

"Dr. Hastings says you have completed all the steps of her program. Obviously, you can attend a meeting any time you feel the need, but she feels you have a good handle on your life and have learned self-control."

I couldn't believe I was actually going to miss Dr. Shirley. "I'd like to think so," I replied, "but what does that mean for me?"

"Your sentence is complete." He grinned wide.

I wilted with relief. "Thank the universe for that."

He chuckled. "You haven't changed one bit, Harmony."

"No Ms. Jones?" I smirked.

"Not this time." His lips tipped up slightly at the corners.

We sat there quietly for a minute in a comfortable silence. Something I never thought I would have with Zander Jackson again.

"Thank you for sending Byron Storm my way," I said quietly, admitting, "he really is the best." And there went that awful lump in my throat again.

"I heard he left. I'm sorry about that. You two seemed... close."

I eyed him curiously. "And you're okay with that?"

"He was never anything official to you. I just sent him your way in case you needed someone to talk to because I wanted you to have the best." He shrugged. "My way of trying to make up for our past."

"I appreciate that, and yes, we got close, but it wasn't meant to be. He's very determined not to cross any lines, official or otherwise."

Zander paused and I didn't think he was going to say anything more, when he finally spoke. "Byron is very loyal. He is passionate about helping people. He didn't tell you about the favor because it involves me, and even today, he is still protecting me. But you deserve to know the truth. I owe you that."

I sat quietly listening, patiently waiting until he was ready to talk, just like Byron used to do with me. Truly listening was an art form very few people had mastered these days, including myself. I was determined to change that going forward.

It would eliminate so many misunderstandings.

"When we were back in college, I was studying to be a lawyer, and he was studying mental health psychology. His family didn't have much. He had a pretty hard life growing up. He was a great tennis player, and that was the help he needed. He earned a scholarship, which was the only way he could go to college. Byron didn't have money, and I did, yet we were the best of friends." Zander shrugged. "Still are."

No matter what had happened between us, I still loved him. My heart ached for all he had gone through as a child. "He never told me about his past or how he grew up."

"It's not something he talks about much. Anyway, he was sweet on the coach's daughter, and she knew it. She led him on. He tried to abstain because he thought it would be crossing a line, but she managed to seduce him. Then she slipped drugs into his drink, knowing the team was having a drug test the next day."

I gasped. "Why would she do that?"

"Because she was sweet on his teammate who was second best to him. The NCAA has a specific banned substance list, and athletes are required to follow their guidelines or risk suspension, loss of eligibility, and more. She was trying to get him kicked off the team so her real love could flourish."

"Oh, no, did Byron lose his scholarship?" I bit my bottom lip.

"No, but he was heartbroken and lost a lot of trust for women."

I nodded. "That explains a lot, but how didn't he get kicked off the team and out of college?"

Zander's eyes locked onto mine. "He felt the side effects from the drugs right away and knew what she had done. He didn't ask, but I insisted. I gave him my urine sample to use because I knew it was clean."

My eyes grew huge. "But that's..."

"More than crossing a line. He knew it put my degree in jeopardy, but I didn't think twice. He would have done the same for me. He's still protecting me by keeping what I did a secret, even from you. He would rather get in trouble himself than put someone he cares about at risk." Zander nodded. "He cares about you, Harm. That's why he didn't want to risk you not making it through this program by crossing any lines."

Oh, Byron, if only you had talked to me. "But he's the one who could have gotten in more serious trouble."

"Like I said, he has always put others first to a fault."

"Thank you for telling me. It explains a lot, but it doesn't really change anything. He still left." I folded my hands because I needed to hold onto something. "I under-stand why a little better now, so I appreciate that."

Zander nodded and stood. "Take care of yourself, Harmony." He pointed at me. "And stay out of trouble."

I gave him a thumb's up and laughed, watching him walk away, then my smile slipped. I hoped Byron didn't see me as trying to sabotage him like his tennis captain's daughter had. No wonder he didn't trust women. If I had known his secret, maybe our conversation would have gone differently.

And I certainly wouldn't have walked away.

Chapter Twenty

June first. A whole new month. A fresh start.

I adjusted the sign on my front door that said, *Grand Reopening!*

The day had finally arrived. The repairs had only taken one month. I was lucky that so many people had banded together to help me. It was heartwarming, yet I had my suspicions they just wanted more witchcraft supplies, judging by the line down the street.

I flipped the sign to *Open* and unlocked the door.

Stepping inside, I nodded to Zoe's daughter, Lexi. She stood behind the counter by the cash register. She was finally old enough, so I had hired her for her very first job. While I appreciated his help, anyone had to be better than my brother Harry.

"The store really looks great, Harm." Zoe joined me near the witchcraft section.

I had redesigned my shop to have an entire wall dedicated to my craft. Out of respect for Phoenix and our newfound truce, I donated my antiques to her shop. She asked me out for coffee next week. She really was just as cool as I had imagined. As for the books, there was no way I was getting rid of my Kama Sutra.

Sorry not sorry, Rose.

"Thanks. I'm pleased with it," I responded to Zoe.

"I love the vibe." Tiffany twirled in a circle. "It's very Zen."

"Agreed." Morti looked around. "Very cool."

"I guess this is it." I nodded. "My life at forty." I smiled. "It's not so bad being me." A small part of me still missed Byron, but I had finally learned I didn't need a man to be happy. I was taking my mother's advice and focusing on me.

Like the fortune cookie had said, *I was in charge of my own happiness...*

And Byron hadn't chosen wisely at the fork in his road. Such is life.

"You rock, girl." Morti gave me her rare Mona Lisa smile.

For the next several hours everyone pitched in and sold out most of my inventory. I would have to start ordering more at this rate. So much had changed since the first of the year. What had started out as an awful rumor hadn't ruined my life after all. My shop was thriving, and I'd chosen to be happy.

So why was there still a missing piece of my heart?

"Thanks so much, Lexi. You did great. I'll see you tomorrow." I closed the door behind her and Zoe, who mouthed, *Thank you.*

They were the last ones to leave.

I locked up and headed upstairs to my apartment. It was an unusually warm evening, so I opened the window to let in a breeze. I inhaled a deep breath...and frowned. Was that smoke? I sniffed again and peeked outside.

A shadow lurked outside my back door, out of the line of my security cameras. The figure was dressed all in black with a hood up and a gas can.

No time to call for help if I wanted to save my store. Grabbing my bat—an upgrade from the broomstick—I ran out my door and down the stairs. Setting my shop and apartment on fire was taking things to a whole new level.

Not on my watch, pal!

Running around the side of my building, I held up my bat and screamed, "Hey! Don't even think about it, Vader! You're messing with the wrong Jedi, and I'm through with you invading my life! The force is definitely not with you this time."

The figure dropped the gas can and started running away.

Dammit! A small fire was burning outside of my building, close to my door. Thank the universe I had opened my window, or I wouldn't have smelled the smoke. If I didn't put the flames out, it would set my building on fire.

Grabbing my hose, I sprayed the fire until the flames

were extinguished. I had seen the person run off. They weren't very fit or fast. Rage filled me, and I couldn't let it go. I had reached my breaking point. Smart or not, I gave chase. It didn't take long to catch up. Lifting my bat, I swung low and hit my target in the leg.

"Ahhh," the person screamed and then toppled to the ground.

Wait a minute...I knew that voice.

Rolling them over, I pulled back their hood.

"Al Shanker?" I pulled out my phone and dialed 911, quickly telling them to send the police, then I hung up even though they told me not to.

I had a beef to settle.

The short, thin man lay in a heap on the ground, whimpering, with blood staining his thinning brown hair from hitting his head on the ground. He kept moaning and rubbing his thigh as he glared up at me.

"You're the one who's been spreading rumors about me and vandalizing my car and shop? Why? What the hell did I ever do to you?"

"That should have been *my* shop," he snarled and tried to get up.

I held my bat higher. "Stay down. What are you talking about?"

"I put in a bid for that shop because it was right across from *Walt's Single Malts*. A smoke shop belongs near a liquor store, not some stupid new age witch crap. You only got that shop cuz your family has pull in this town. It should have been mine."

"So, you were going to burn it down?" I sneered at him. "You're crazy. I was in my apartment above the store. You could have killed me."

The first police car on the scene was Officer Pickles. He got out of his car and walked over to me. "Harm, put down the bat and tell me what's going on here."

"Not until you arrest him."

His eyes widened when he spotted Al. "For what?"

"He's the person spreading the rumors, Don. He vandalized my car and my shop because he wanted to move his cigar shop to my space. He knows my building, so he knew how to avoid the cameras, but I caught him in the act. He tried to burn down my shop with me in it. The evidence is still outside the back door."

Pickles told another officer to check it out while he helped Al to his feet. "I have to say I'm disappointed in you, Al. You make one hell of a cigar. It didn't matter where your shop was located." He shook his head at the man with disgust. "Such a pity."

"It mattered to me." Al thrust his chin out, his eyes looking crazier than the rumors he'd spread.

"Well, now you'll have plenty of time to think about it in jail."

"Spreading rumors isn't a crime."

Pickles face soured. "No, but vandalism is...and so is attempted arson."

Al's face paled as Pickles put him in cuffs and helped him into his patrol car. Shutting the door, he faced me. "Do me a favor?"

"What's that?"

"Don't play cops and robbers again, please." Don adjusted his hat. "Lolita doesn't like gray hair, and you're giving me plenty."

"Done." I dropped my bat, exhausted.

"You need a ride?"

"Are you kidding? I'm sure half the town knows what happened by now. My father and brothers will be here in," I looked at my watch, "five, four, three, two...and there they are." My father and brothers might have tried to make me tough, but I would never stop being their baby girl. To say they were fiercely protective would be an understatement.

Everything happened at once.

My mother inspected every inch of me.

My brothers held my father back from killing Al.

Pickles hauled Al away...

And Byron Stone appeared before me in the flesh.

I COULDN'T BELIEVE Byron was sitting on my couch in my living room, sipping whiskey. He looked thinner and tired. His hair needed a trim. He needed to shave. Yet I'd never seen anyone more beautiful in my life.

It took some convincing to get my father and brothers to let Byron take me home, but in the end, they respected my wishes. My mother told me not to take any shit—her words not mine—and then she hugged me tight.

I'd never loved her more.

I'd ridden with Byron back to my place, and every part of me homed in on him and his energy. I swear I could hear his heartbeat from where I sat in the passenger seat of his '71 Mustang. A kaleidoscope of emotions swirled within my core. I had so much to say, but I wasn't sure he would want to hear it. Neither one of us had spoken the entire ride. When he put the car in park, I couldn't help myself and invited him up.

He nodded an affirmative and followed me inside.

I kept my breathing calm and assured myself that no matter what happened tonight, I was a better person because of Byron. Yet there was a part of my heart that prayed that him coming all the way back to Mayflower truly meant something. While I turned on some lights and grabbed us a couple beers, he silently made himself at home.

Grabbing a throw, I wrapped it around myself and joined him on the couch. It was strange. I wasn't mad at him. I was sad yet grateful to see his face again. All I wanted was closure so maybe, just maybe, I could finally forget about him.

Taking a page from his book, I sat quietly and waited for him to speak.

"You look good, Harmony." He smiled tenderly at me when he finally spoke.

"Thank you. I feel good. I finished my sentence and had my grand reopening. And now I've put a stop to the rumors once and for all. Life is good. I have everything I could want." *Liar.* "You look tired."

"I am." He ran a hand over his face. "I'm sorry I didn't call."

I believed him. "Why didn't you?"

"I never told you how I grew up. My father left us when we were little, and my mother raised my sisters and me by herself. She never remarried, working two, sometimes three jobs just to make ends meet. We didn't have much, and life wasn't easy, but we always felt loved because of her. She means everything to me."

"I get it. My mother and I might have had our differences, but I still love her. I took your advice, and we talked. Things are so much better now."

"I'm glad. That bond is so important. That's why when I got the phone call that my mother had a heart attack, I dropped everything and went home."

I sucked in a sharp breath. "Oh, no. I'm so sorry. Is she okay?"

"She will be. It's been a rough month. My sisters and I have been taking turns at the rehab center while she is recovering."

I closed my eyes for a moment, realizing it must have been his sister who answered the phone.

"It was the widowmaker. She should be dead. She got lucky." His pained gaze met mine, and I felt every bit of his sorrow. "I should have called, but all I could focus on was keeping my mother alive."

"You did the right thing. She's your mother. I'm just—"

"The woman I love."

My heart flipped over, and I gaped at him. I couldn't

have heard him right. "W-What did you just say?" I whispered, afraid to speak too loudly and wake up from this dream.

"You heard me right." His voice softened and for once, his blank face was full of expression. I could see everything he was feeling as clearly as the moon saw the stars. "I have been so in love with you for a very long time, Harmony Jones."

"But Zander told me your secret. How that awful girl tried to ruin you, and then I went and almost ruined you, too." My voice cracked and this time I let the tears flow. "How can you even trust me anymore?"

"Because you're not her, and you didn't ruin me." He gently swiped my tears away with his thumb. "I was trying to protect you."

I put my hand over his and held on tight. "You need to stop protecting people and start protecting yourself."

"I know your life is great right now, and you don't have any reason to forgive me for leaving without saying goodbye, but I've been miserable without you." He brought my hand to his lips and kissed it softly. "I can't imagine living my life without you in it, but I will if that's what you want." His face pinched, and his voice filled with pain as he asked, "Are you saying you don't love me back?"

"For once in your life, stop worrying about what other people want. What do you want, Byron?"

His gaze blazed into mine. "I want you."

I threw myself into his arms. "Then I'm yours, babe."

"Does this mean you still love me, my princess?"

"You know it! And this time I'm never letting you go, Han." We both met in the middle and kissed each other this time, with all the passion and love we felt as we headed to our very own galaxy far away from our lonely pasts and a promise of eternity.

Books By Kari Lee Townsend

KALLI BALLAS MYSTERY

Mind Over Murder

Two Cents of Doom

A Touch of Malice

An Inkling of Evil

Mayhem on the Mind

CECE MONROE MYSTERY

Harmful Habits

SUNNY MEADOWS MYSTERY

Tempest in the Tea Leaves

Corpse in the Crystal Ball

Trouble in the Tarot

Shenanigans in the Shadows

Perish in the Palm

Hazard in the Horoscope

Chaos and Cold Feet

Murder in the Meditation

Cruising into Danger

Road Trip to Ruin

<u>DIGITAL DIVA</u>

Talk to the Hand

Rise of the Phenoteens

Books By Kari Lee Harmon

COLDWATER COVE

Dark Seas

Frozen Waters

Dangerous Thaw

Deadly Frost

STANDALONE NOVELS

Valley of Secrets

Until Tomorrow

Project Produce

Love Lessons

LAKEHOUSE TREASURES NOVELLAS

James

Amber

Meghan

Brook

MERRY SCROOG-MAS NOVELLAS

Naughty or Nice

Sleigh Bells Ring

Jingle all the Way

<u>TRIPLE R RANCH SHORT STORIES</u>

Destiny Wears Spurs

Spurred by Fate

<u>PORTRAIT OF A WOMAN</u>

Resilient

Resourceful

Rebellious

About the Author

Kari Lee Townsend is a National Bestselling Author of mysteries & a tween superhero series. She also writes romance and women's fiction as Kari Lee Harmon. With a background in English education, she's now a full-time writer, wife to her own superhero, mom of 3 sons, 1 darling diva, 1 daughter-in-law & 3 lovable fur babies. These days you'll find her walking her dogs or hard at work on her next story, living a blessed life.